DAI
His Journey

Mark Moriarty

© 2024, Mark Moriarty (text and images)

ISBN: 978-1-7637145-0-2

The moral right of the author has been asserted.

All rights reserved. No part of this publication may be reproduced, distributed, or transmitted in any form or by any means, including photocopying, recording, or other electronic or mechanical methods, without the prior written permission of the author.

Permission granted for fair use and criticism.

First

The sun was shining when Dahlin walked out of his shelter. He yawned and thought to himself, "Was this to be my day?" He had thought this every morning since he had woken up, with a sore head, under a tree a year ago. He only remembered his name and that he could read and write. But despite this mystery he felt peaceful. He always began each day hopefully.

Dahlin was young and short, with a mop of thick brown hair on his head and with a face that gave others a sunny smile. His arms and legs were stout and stocky, and he was agile and strong.

He looked around for food. Not far from his shelter was an Orange tree with its fruit hanging from the branches. He walked over to it and pulled a few off the tree. He peeled a little of the skin off one to reveal a couple juicy pieces. Dahlin ate these two and put the rest into his backpack. He wondered why it was called an Orange, perhaps because it was orange?

Dahlin was always ready to shift home. He carried two sets of clothing, both the same. These were green long-sleeved shirts with two breast pockets; and green trousers with four pockets, two in the front and two in the back. He had one pair of boots which were wearing out. On his back, he carried a pack that stowed his spare clothes, a small axe, used for building his shelters, and a water flask made from leathery leaves sealed by heated rocks. Around his waist, he carried a pouch for his food to eat while he walked.

Dahlin was in search of a place called Hermitage. He did not know very much about it, but he knew he had to get there. Whenever he met anyone, he would ask them if they knew anything about it. Often what they said was not encouraging. Some people thought it was far away, others thought it was only a legend. The only thing Dahlin knew was that it was somewhere north.

Today he had to find a village and get a job. He needed new boots. When the ground was hard his boots were letting in too many stones and when the path was wet, after rain, his boots let in water. He knew that having damp feet was not the best.

He moved off through the trees and found a path leading to a village. It was a well-worn dry path, and the stones hurt his feet. Along the side of the track, flowers were blooming. Their beauty and liveliness cheered him up. He liked flowers, their presence created a feeling of hopefulness.

The birds started to sing and flew down to perch on his shoulders and outstretched hand. He did not know why but the little birds always liked to greet him this way. He enjoyed singing with them and forgot his sore feet.

It took several hours to reach the village, but he was not tired. He had a purpose, and this gave him strength.

On reaching the village he walked down the Main Street. Several people smiled and said hello, except the people who kept their hands in their pockets and hardly raised their eyes from the ground. Accidentally one of these people bumped into Dahlin.

"Hey, what's the matter with you?" The man started to say, but when he saw Dahlin's eyes, he stopped speaking.

"Excuse me," said Dahlin. "Do you know where the carpenter is in this village?"

"Yes," the man replied hesitantly, "his name is Johan."

The man gave Dahlin directions and slowly walked away, looking back several times and almost ran into a tree.

Johan was just closing his shop door when Dahlin arrived.

"Oh, excuse me, sir. My name is Dahlin. I was wondering if you could give me a job for a little while. My boots are wearing out and my feet are sore. I do very much need a new pair of boots."

Johan looked at Dahlin and said, "I have many travellers who come and go asking for jobs. I find them irresponsible. But you look like you can be trusted. Come in, I will show you what to do."

Dahlin was so excited he grabbed Johan's hand and shook it enthusiastically.

"Well, there's no need for that," Johan said as he strangely, reluctantly pulled his hand from Dahlin. "You can start now, while I go down the street for half an hour."

Johan had several long pieces of wood he wanted cut to make the legs of a table. Dahlin expertly cut them to the correct length.

Johan returned within the half hour and set to work constructing a table. It was for the baker and needed to be strong.

"Why don't you go outside and cut some wood for the fire? We will need it tonight. It's going to be cold," directed Johan. "The axe is in the hut near the back fence."

"Certainly," said Dahlin, "anything to make you happy." He got up and walked outside.

Johan stopped his work and looked after him.

"What is this young person doing?" he wondered. "And where has he been?" Johan decided to ask Dahlin to stay with him. "I could make up a mat bed on the floor," he said to himself.

Outside, Dahlin had a question of his own. "I wonder if the carpenter will let me sleep on the floor?"

From the carpenter's house to the back shed was a short path covered by woodchips. Next to the shed was the wood stack. It was quite full as Johan had just finished a wood drive for the coming winter.

Dahlin pulled open the shed door and saw the axe. As he reached for it, he was suddenly startled by a black spider that fell onto his hand. The spider froze, as did Dahlin, then quick as a flash it ran up Dahlin's arm but stopped at Dahlin's elbow.

If one could see the spider's eyes, one would have been surprised by their expression. It looked up into Dahlin's eyes then dropped to the floor.

Dahlin relieved to be free of the spider, grabbed the axe and quickly went outside. The little scare gave him the energy to chop quite a lot of wood. As he worked, little birds flew down from the trees and perched on the log pile and sang to him. This made him feel better.

Back in the house, Johan prepared the food for the evening meal. Through the window, he could see the sun setting. A beautiful, powerful red with springing arms of gold.

Then a strange thing happened. He saw Dahlin

as he walked along the path, arms full of wood. He reached a spot where the setting sun was at his back and stopped. He turned around to gaze at it for a while. Johan saw something he did not believe possible.

The golden rays of the sun seemed to bend toward Dahlin in a soothing, caring embrace. Johan was amazed by this touching scene and felt it deeply in his heart. The sun was shining love through his window. For the few moments it lasted, he felt enchanted. Dahlin moved on. Very suddenly a pang of fear stung his heart, and then it disappeared. He would ponder both feelings for quite some time.

"Would you open the door, please?" called Dahlin. Johan startled, leapt up and let Dahlin in.

"I hope I have chopped enough wood for you," said Dahlin, as he placed the stack by the fire.

"Yes, yes, that looks plenty," replied Johan feeling warmly happy again. "Now, what would you like to eat, I have plenty?"

"Oh! I didn't think I was staying for a meal," said Dahlin, embarrassed.

"Of course, you must, you should, I would love to have you as my guest. It isn't often I have visitors. My son has left me, and I rarely have someone good to talk to," insisted Johan.

"Well, if you think you will enjoy my company. I know I will enjoy yours," replied Dahlin.

"Yes, yes, good, and later we can talk by the fire,

and you can sleep in the house," enthused Johan.

"Oh, thank you so much." Dahlin was very pleased to have a roof over his head not made of leaves and branches.

After their meal, Dahlin and Johan sat by the fireplace. Dahlin sat close with his arms around his legs and watched the flames spring and dance.

Johan sat on his favourite chair also looking at the fire. The silence was very warming like the heat from the hearth. He looked over at Dahlin and wondered if he dared ask him a few questions.

"What do you see in the flickering flames," he asked, without realising he spoke. An uneasiness gripped him that he was trespassing on someone else's dreams.

"Oh, I see many things," Dahlin replied without looking up, unaware of Johan's embarrassment. "I see my future. The place I am longing to find. The flames dance with love and joy feeding on the endless wood of everyone's co-operation and respect for each other. I see the sages who have searched the books of wisdom that guide us to discover our true selves. I find completeness, excitement and contentment, where no one is afraid to be themselves."

Johan was amazed at this insight and asked, "And what is this place called?"

"I'm not sure really," Dahlin looked up at Johan. "People have called it Hermitage, but I think that's just an expression for what it does to someone."

"Hermitage," Johan pondered aloud. "I have heard that name before."

"You have? Where, who by? Please tell me," Dahlin asked excitedly.

"Well, now, calm down Dahlin, calm down," Johan's thoughts were racing. "I've only heard people speak about it mockingly. A dream place, that doesn't exist. Or it is so far south or north, nobody here could reach it."

"Oh," said Dahlin deflated, "I've heard that before," and he returned to gaze into the flames of his dreams.

Johan rested for a few minutes. He wanted to know more out about Dahlin, so he asked, "I'm sorry, I don't know very much about Hermitage, but tell me, where do you come from and why would such a young lad as you have such a curiosity?"

Dahlin kept looking at the fire. He did not speak for a minute. Johan felt lonely again.

"I'm sorry," replied Dahlin, as he looked up into Johan's eyes. "I get too excited. I should have realised you would know nothing about Hermitage."

He paused and looked around the room. Shadows of many things danced by the light of the fire.

"You have been here a long time, I see," said Dahlin.

"Yes, I have," replied Johan, wondering why Dahlin had avoided answering his question.

"I feel very tired, I have had a hard day. I will tell you tomorrow night what you would like to know about me. Until the morning, good night." And to Johan's surprise, Dahlin fell fast asleep, curled up on the mat by the fire.

"This is surely the strangest person I have ever met," Johan said to himself. He got up and went to his bedroom, He took one of his blankets and carefully placed it over Dahlin.

As he did this the fire flame's light created a warm friendly expression on Dahlin's face. Johan stared for longer than he realised. When he retired to his bed, he felt extremely comforted. A part of his loneliness was taken away.

The morning sun crept over the horizon peeking at the sparkling jewels hanging from branches and resting on the ground. It was a beautiful sight. The shimmering green of dew flooded the morning light. And suddenly, as if from nowhere, swam a dancer. He twirled and leapt, ran and jumped his morning dance of joy. It was Dahlin.

Dahlin, catching crisp breaths of the morning air, danced to each bush, tree and flower around the carpenter's yard. It was a strong dance, full of energy and emotion. Seldom had Dahlin felt so overcome with feelings of mystery, that he had to dance to express it vividly.

He stopped by a tree and the birds in its branches were singing. Dahlin sang with them this song.

Dahlin's Song

Some things stand where they're never used
Collecting dust and staying very new
If someone would pick them up
And try to find what they are for
He may discover they're no use
So, they are left again, dusty poor.
I am looking for dreams that are real
I know I'll find them that's how I feel
When one day I will see
The mountain standing where it has been
Then I know I've found all my dreams
And rest secure with all I've seen.

When he had finished Dahlin stayed to watch the sun complete its rise. He felt more alive now than he ever had before. Perhaps he was close. He did not know but he was feeling something new.

Dahlin collected an armful of logs and went back to the carpenter's house. The carpenter was up preparing breakfast.

"Where have you been?" he asked.

"Oh, just watching the sunrise," replied Dahlin. Then he added. "And I thought we needed some more wood."

Dahlin dropped the wood on the rack next to the fire.

"Good, thank you," said Johan. "I hope you like bread and eggs, it's all I have."

"Yes," said Dahlin, very pleased.

As they settled down to their meal, Johan asked, "What else were you doing outside? I thought I heard someone singing."

"Really," answered Dahlin. "I guess it must have been me. I felt very good this morning, so I thought I would express it with a dance and a song. It's not often I get the impulse to do such things."

"Well, be careful, some people might think you're strange," said Johan. Then upon reflection added. "But then, I suppose it isn't a bad idea."

They finished breakfast and began their work for the day. Dahlin liked working for Johan, and Johan enjoyed the company. Since his wife had died, he had missed having a friendly presence in his house.

The following afternoon the baker, Fruro, arrived to collect the table he had ordered.

He said on seeing it, "A fine piece of craftsmanship, excellent work Johan. You've earned every coin it's going to cost me."

Fruro laughed, he was a portly man. To Dahlin, it looked like a shaking pumpkin.

"The legs of the table look especially well made too," continued Fruro.

"Dahlin made those," Johan informed him.

Fruro looked at Dahlin and smiled broadly.

"A very good job, young fellow. Where have you come from? I've never seen you before."

"That's a long story," started Dahlin.

"Well, I haven't time for long stories," interrupted Fruro. "I've got to get back to the bakery. Give me a hand with the table young fellow."

Dahlin helped carry the table back to the bakery. Fruro had an old table in the middle of the room that had to be removed before they could put the new table in its place. They had the new table in place by noon. Dahlin was feeling hungry. He was not used to the hard work of shifting heavy things around.

"Well," laughed Fruro. "It looks really good. Now when I thump the dough, everything won't shake so much." He laughed again.

Dahlin thought that the only thing that would shake would be Fruro's stomach!

On his way back to Johan's shop, Dahlin nibbled on the bun Fruro had given him. It was delicious so he wanted to enjoy it slowly.

Several birds flew down and sang to Dahlin. People who passed by were amazed at the behaviour of the birds, but when they saw Dahlin give the birds crumbs from his bun, they thought that was the reason for their songs. Little did they realise they sang for no reward, but because they wanted to sing for Dahlin.

Dahlin worked the rest of the day with Johan, the carpenter. When evening came, he went outside to the wood pile and cut some more logs for the evening's fire.

He chopped enough for one armful and as he was gathering the logs, the spider, from the night before, dropped down from above onto the logs.

Dahlin was surprised and almost dropped the wood. The spider gave Dahlin a very strange look. Dahlin sensed it as a warning. But what kind of warning? He realised that he would have to be more careful.

Having given his warning message, the spider jumped off the logs and scurried off into the wood heap. Dahlin walked thoughtfully back to the house.

Johan had their dinner prepared and Dahlin felt glad to have some nourishment to feed the day's labour.

Later that evening they were sitting by the fire.

"Can you tell me about your son, Johan?" asked Dahlin.

"My son has gone away," sighed Johan.

"Yes, I know, but what was he like?" replied Dahlin.

"Well, Dahlin, my son Rensin and I never really got on well together. He always opposed everything I wanted to do. We would argue and fight so much that I could never make him see reason. Anyway, he left me a few years ago."

"Do you ever think he will return?" asked Dahlin, feeling sorry for Johan.

"Yes, I'm afraid he will," answered Johan, and with that, went off to bed.

The next morning Johan was in a quiet mood. But as the day progressed, he returned to his friendly self whenever around Dahlin or when he watched him work.

During the afternoon Dahlin went to see Callum, the cobbler. His shop was not far from Johan's carpentry.

On entering the shop, a bell rang from atop the door. Callum was working at his bench and stopped what he was doing and impatiently turned around to see who had disturbed his labours. He was about to say angrily, "What do you want you little ...." But stopped himself when he saw Dahlin's face.

"Er, what can I do for you, my kind little fellow?" he said instead. He was surprised at what he said, as he never gave compliments to strangers.

"Would you be so kind as to make me a strong pair of boots. They would need to be suitable for walking on roads and paths that will be rough, stony and wet?" Dahlin asked.

"Yes, I can do that," he replied to Dahlin.

He then called out to his wife, "Sharin, my dear, would you please come and take the details for this boot-making order?" He thought to himself, "I haven't called her 'dear' in a long time."

Sharin came into the shop from out the back and smiled at her husband, then looked at Dahlin for few moments.

"Let's get some particulars for the boots you would like made, shall we?" she said to Dahlin with a big, sweet smile. Upon seeing Dahlin she remembered the joy of her children.

"I need boots that are very strong, good for walking over hills and rough roads and for where there are no roads. The ones I have now are wearing thin and short for my feet. I think my feet have grown along with the rest of me." Dahlin laughed.

"Then we need to take some measurements and decide on the materials required. We will have to get some special leather from the Leathery in the next town but that will only take a few days. Are you in a hurry for them?" she asked.

"No. I am happy to wait until they are ready. How much will they cost me?" Dahlin inquired.

At this, Sharin had to think. It had not occurred to her that she would charge Dahlin for the boots. What a funny thing to think she thought. She wrote a figure on a piece of paper and gave it to Dahlin.

"That's a generous price. I am happy to pay that as I am working for Johan, the carpenter, and I have saved enough from my wages," he replied.

"Ah, Johan," she remarked, "a lovely man and a hard worker. It was sad about his wife and terrible about his son. Did he talk about what happened?" she asked.

"I think he is reluctant to talk about his sorrow, so I haven't persisted in any questioning," replied Dahlin politely.

"Yes, a good way to act. Not me, though, I would like to know more. I'm a bit too inquisitive. Oh, I let that slip out, didn't I?" she embarrassingly admitted. "I'll let you know when you can come in for a fitting," she continued.

Dahlin gave her a happy smile and left the shop. Sharin turned towards her husband and said, "What a gentle little soul he is. I wonder where he comes from?" Her husband did not reply but gave her a loving smile and a sigh.

While he waited for his new boots to be made, Dahlin continued to work for Johan, who found him a willing and clever worker. Johan thought he could become an excellent carpenter, but it seemed that Dahlin was not interested.

Johan asked him, "Would you like to become my apprentice? I can see that your skills have increased in the time you have been with me. What is it now, about two weeks? You complete your constructions, chairs, tables and implements efficiently and my customers have been very happy with their purchases. Some even give me extra and have told their friends who have now come asking for things to be made or mended. So, what do you think?"

Dahlin paused and looked up from the chair he was mending.

He replied, "Yes, that is true. I feel my capabilities and skills at rendering wood have improved quickly. But that is the way with me. I learn very quickly and enjoy what I do. But, sadly, Johan, carpentry is not for me. I have another task that aches in my heart and soul and will not give me rest until it has been accomplished. I will work for you until my new pair of boots are ready. I have already had one fitting and Callum has said they will be ready soon. I need a strong and durable pair of boots, and they are costly due to the special leather required. I have saved enough to buy them from your kind wages."

Johan was disappointed but knew that it was impossible to persuade Dahlin to change his mind. As kind and gentle as Dahlin was, there was a determination, fortitude, and strength in him that did not fear the future.

A few days later Dahlin paid Callum for his new boots. He was very happy with them, they felt comfortable but also strong. The following day he said his farewells to Johan.

"I thank you most heartedly for your kindness. I wish you well and that your sorrows find a resolution that gives you peace. I fear, though, that you may have to endure a little more pain before that is to happen. I know we will meet again, so I will not say goodbye but farewell." Dahlin said these words looking directly into Johan's eyes.

Johan was surprised by these prophetic words but felt a sense that they would come true sooner than he expected. He wanted to make peace with his son but did not know how that would be achieved. Hope does not always know how its desire is fulfilled.

"I wish you well, my dear little fellow. I am sure, too, that we will meet again. I thank you for the peace of mind you have given me. I will miss you around the shop as you have been one of my best workers as well as a new friend. Until we meet again, farewell." Johan almost cried when he said these words to Dahlin.

Dahlin shook his hand, gathered up his pack, turned and walked out of the village without turning back.

On his way towards the road out of the town, Dahlin walked by the cobbler's shop and decided to go in and say goodbye. Sharin greeted him heartedly.

"My little friend, you appear to be on your way, is that so?" she asked.

"Yes," replied Dahlin. "My time has come to leave, and I will put your boots to a good test," he joked.

"Ha, ha," laughed Sharin. "But before you go, I must get you some food for your journey. You may not reach another town for some distance." She left and entered her kitchen.

Callum came into the shop and saw Dahlin, and greeted him with a smile.

"You are heading into some change in the

weather, I fear," informed Callum.

"I have walked through much worse," smiled Dahlin.

Sharin came in from the kitchen and handed Dahlin a bag with bread and fruit.

"This should feed you for a few days. I wish you all the best and hope to see you again someday," she said.

"Thank you with my blessing. I may return so I will be delighted to see you again. Farewell." Dahlin gave them a beautiful smile and a cheery wave as he continued on his way.

A few days later a man entered the town from the opposite direction and walked briskly towards the carpenter's shop. Above him flew three ravens uttering their 'arrr' hoarse call to each other.

Johan was working at his bench when a dark shadow eclipsed the light of his door. He turned and gasped at the person standing at the entrance.

"Rensin," Johan breathed. "What brings you back?"

Rensin was tall, angular, and strong with a handsome but fierce face.

"Nothing brings me 'back'," Rensin harshly replied. "I am on the trail of someone, and it has brought me here." He looked around the workshop. "I sense something different in this room. Have you had a visitor?" Rensin questioned menacingly.

Johan was not afraid of his son but knew that he was never inclined to good, answered cautiously, without lying.

"I had a new worker here for a couple of weeks, but he left, he was a good helper." He eyed his son as he gave this answer.

"What was his name? Was he short? Was he friendly? Which way did he go?" retorted Rensin.

"His name is not important, neither is his destination. I keep my confidences." Johan replied firmly.

"Ah, you have told me little but enough for me to know he was here. I will find him and bring him sadness." Rensin answered as he walked to Johan's bench, picked up the hammer, felt its clawed head and muttered. "Just like my pets."

Suddenly, he threw the hammer to the floor, hurriedly turned without looking at his father, and left the shop and walked in the direction Dahlin had taken.

Second

Dahlin walked for a couple of days along the road but felt he had to follow the next path that came his way. It was not long before a narrow path appeared to his right and he walked along that and soon he was surrounded by trees. The path grew undulating and steep. It became rocky and he was pleased his new boots supported him to walk without getting sore feet.

It started to get dark, and a little rain was falling. Dahlin needed shelter but found no place of cover. As he turned the next bend he saw a house, but there was no light from its windows. He approached cautiously just as the rain became heavier. He looked through the window near the front door but could not see inside. He knocked on the door and it opened as if to welcome a tired traveller.

He entered and called out, "Is there anyone here? Is it alright if I take shelter from the approaching storm?" There was no reply.

He felt assured there was no one in the small house and started looking around. There were only three main rooms: a room with a fireplace, a kitchen, and a bedroom with one bed covered by a straw mattress. The fireplace had some dry wood and kindling so Dahlin quickly got a fire going and warmed himself for a few minutes wondering who left the wood. He decided he would replenish whatever he burnt for whoever came after him. Perhaps this house was left unlocked for any weary traveller to rest.

He went into the kitchen. It had a table with four chairs. Over the basin was a water pump which upon pumping squirted out fresh water. He used his cup to fill his flask as he did not know where he would find water again as he was unfamiliar with the countryside. He thought that whoever built the house knew that there was water below. Perhaps the house was built over a well. He felt blessed that he had come upon the house just as he needed a place for shelter.

Dahlin sat at the table and ate a little of the bread and a piece of fruit that Sharin had kindly given him. It made him feel happy that there were people in the world who cared for others with no thought of reward.

What Dahlin did not realise yet was that it was something in his presence that brought out the best in people but also, unfortunately, the worst in some too.

It was getting late, and the storm was still raging outside as if in a warning that trouble was not far behind. He went into the bedroom and sat on the mattress then noticed there was a small table by the bed.

He stood up and discovered an old map on the table. It showed where he was and the town where he stayed. He did not realise that the town's name was Sunatin. The map showed several other towns and the roads and paths connecting them. It also depicted all the forests and mountains that Dahlin would have to cross on his journey. Then to his surprise, he discovered the map showed him the location of Hermitage. It was a distance away and would not be easy to reach. Instead of making him excited it seemed to calm his spirits and gave him a sense of hope. His weariness then took over and Dahlin fell on the bed into a peaceful sleep.

Through the window three little birds looked at him as they sheltered from the rain. They would soon become his companions and protectors.

Just before sunrise, Dahlin awoke feeling refreshed and energised for his day of walking. He went outside and waited for the sunrise. Above him in a tree, the three little birds watched. As the sun rose, he breathed deeply and sang his song of praise and felt blessed. Returning to the house he washed his face in the kitchen and ate some more of the food Sharin had given him. He went into the bedroom to get his backpack and decided to take the map for he felt it was left here to guide him on his journey. He folded it carefully and put it into one of the pockets of his backpack. He then swung the pack onto his back and walked out of the house. He left the door unlocked as it was when he entered.

He found the path again and walked steadily for an hour when he came to a stream. The water felt refreshing as he took some to drink and filled up his flask. He looked for a place to cross and noticed the three birds flying around stepping stones over the stream. He thought, "I think the birds have found a way for me to get across the stream without me getting myself wet, how amazing."

As he walked across the stones the three little birds hovered a little above his head as if making sure Dahlin did not slip into the water.

He followed the path again as it led towards a forest in the distance. The three little birds followed.

Dahlin walked all day along the path and in the late afternoon reached the forest. He stopped to check the map. It showed that he had not gone far from the stream. This gave him an indication of distance and how far away Hermitage was from his present position. He sat beneath a tree and pondered about what to do.

The three little birds were perched on a branch just above his head. He looked up and said, "Hello my little friends. Are you following me or guiding me?"

They sang to him a lovely song. Dahlin was able to understand their song and it filled him with delight and reassurance.

"I hope you stay with me my little birds and become my companions if it pleases you," invited Dahlin. He never felt coercion was a way to make friends.

The little birds tweeted "yes" in reply.

That night Dahlin found a hewn-out tree trunk which was ideal for cover and protection from the night. The three little birds now felt so safe around

Dahlin that they joined him there. He gave them some of his bread to eat and they chirpily gave thanks as they ate.

Dahlin settled down to sleep using his backpack as a pillow. As he slept, the little birds took turns looking out into the darkness for any dangers. There were none, yet.

Dahlin was awakened by birdsong. The three little birds were singing their praises at the rising sun. Dahlin joined them with his song. It filled them all with hope and delight. Dahlin knew that the sun was just a huge fiery ball a great distance away but closer than all the other stars that it resembled. His delight in it was that he knew it was given to this world by someone far greater, the One who created all. It was a gift of love.

After a little breakfast the four travellers kept to the path, one walking, three flying. They encountered no one else on their way which Dahlin felt was strange. Perhaps there was something in the forest that was fearful. He felt no fear himself and the little birds trusted in Dahlin.

That night they found another tree for shelter. They enjoyed some food to eat and songs to sing. It was getting cold.

This same pattern of their journey continued for several more days. Dahlin wondered if they would ever find anything. The map did not indicate any inhabitants on the path they were travelling. They rested again for the night in a shallow cave.

About noon the next day, they came upon a log house with smoke billowing from its chimney.

"Well, my little friends, we have found someone," he said to the birds. "Let's hope he is friendly," he cautioned.

The little birds flew quickly to the window of the house and looked in. They saw a very old man in a rocking chair by the fire.

He looked up and saw the birds, raised his hand and waved to them. The birds darted back to Dahlin and sang to him a happy tune. Dahlin knew that this meant it was safe for him to knock on the door.

Dahlin knocked three times on the door and heard the old man call out, "Come in and be not a stranger."

Dahlin entered and the old man welcomed him with a smile and a question, "My name is Haran, what is your name my little man?"

"My name is Dahlin, thank you for letting me into your dwelling and out of the cold. Your fire's heat has already warmed me as has your welcome," replied Dahlin cheerfully.

"I have lived here many a year. I used to be a mountaineer and travelled everywhere over this land. But now I am old and tired and have few visitors and now I know you will be my last," predicted Haran.

Dahlin pondered for a few seconds on Haran's words but asked him instead, "I am searching for Hermitage, and I found a map showing it is in the mountains. Do you know of it?" inquired Dahlin.

"Ha, ha," laughed Haran. "Young people like to ask their questions and inquiries quickly but first we will have something to eat. I am sure you are hungry."

"Yes, I am," replied Dahlin. "I also have three friends who would delight in some little food too."

"You are referring, I guess, to the three little birds who spied me through the window. Yes, let them in if they are comfortable being in an enclosed room," invited Haran.

Dahlin went to the door and opened it. The three little birds eagerly flew in from the cold and perched on a chair near the table. They looked around and chirped cheerfully.

"It would seem they trust you. I have learnt they are a very intelligent trio," stated Dahlin.

"I give no harm to anyone, and especially I feel that way towards you and your companions which is something I have never felt before. Even though I am old and have had many adventures and encounters, it is refreshing to feel something new," confessed Haran.

Haran prepared some soup and stew with bread which proved to be a very satisfying meal. The three little birds enjoyed Haran's bread, which surprised them by its flavour and texture, that they sang a joyful song in thanks.

"I thank you my new little friends for your joyous appreciation of my humble food," then turning to Dahlin, Haran asked, "Show me the map and I may be able to help you find your way for I have been over all this land and have been near to the place you seek, Hermitage."

Dahlin quickly took the map from his backpack and spread it out over the table.

Haran looked at the map intently and traced his finger on many of the roads and paths. He then closed his eyes for a while and breathed a sigh of satisfaction.

"This is my map. I drew it during the many years I transversed this land. It will give you much help in finding your way, but it is not as detailed as I would have liked it to be, as many things cannot be marked on a map. You will discover those for yourself," he advised Dahlin.

"I am truly surprised and delighted to meet the maker of this map," responded Dahlin, "but how did it find its way to the house in which I found it, several days' distance from here?"

"It was stolen by a beggar many years ago. I befriended him but he was ungrateful and left during the night. I discovered he had stolen my food and this map. Not all my guests have been as friendly as you and your birds," said Haran sadly recalling this betrayal.

"Your story only tells part of the events. How did it end up in that house for me to find?" questioned Dahlin.

"We never know all the happenings of the past, but it worked out well, didn't it? You found it then it led you to me. We must be happy with that," counselled Haran.

"I accept the truth of that, and I am pleased that we can return it to you," replied Dahlin.

"Oh no, my new friend, it is yours to keep. You will need it. I no longer have use of it as I will be a traveller no more. My days are now to sit by the fire, tend my little garden and wait for you to return to tell me of your adventures," encouraged Haran.

He smiled at Dahlin who returned a wide smile of thanks and a little laugh. The three little birds chirped happily too.

They talked the afternoon away about Haran's journeys but little of Dahlin's quest. Finally, at the table for the evening meal, Dahlin questioned Haran some more.

"You have placed on the map, Hermitage, a far distance from here. This is the place I seek. Did you explore it, what did you find or discover?"

"That was not so long ago. I saw Hermitage from afar, but it was high in the mountain, and I was not able to reach it as the way up to it was steep, rocky, and surrounded by dense vegetation," replied Haran.

"How did you know it was Hermitage? Was there a sign or marker?" inquired Dahlin.

"There was nothing to mark its name. I just knew," was Haran's strange reply.

"You leave me with puzzling thoughts," Dahlin said quietly. "I feel sure though that I will reach it and discover its mysteries."

Haran looked at Dahlin for a few moments then smiled and nodded in agreement. "Yes, I am sure you will."

Dahlin slept the night by the fire. The birds took turns watching over him.

Dahlin woke to a cloudy sky and was unable to welcome the sunrise. This did not bother him for in his heart he still sang his song of praise.

Haran prepared them a little breakfast and while eating Dahlin said, "We will continue our journey today following your map. It has helped to give us hope that we will find Hermitage very shortly."

"That pleases me," replied Haran. "I have something for you that you may need in case you come across danger, or danger comes across you."

He walked over to a large trunk and pulled out a shining sword. He swung it through the air, and it sang its deadly song. The three little birds were amazed and frightened by the sound and flew away from it to the door. Haran then handed it to Dahlin.

Dahlin looked up at him and said, "I am most grateful that you would offer me a gift for my protection, but I must refuse it. Never have I handled a sword and never am I willing to," he said kindly. "You must fear that danger is going to meet us on our path."

"Yes, yes, there will be danger," Haran warned, "you must have a way to protect yourself," he urged.

"I am sure that there will be danger but there are other ways to find defence against it. I will trust in that, I always have, and safety will be given me," Dahlin tried to reassure him.

Haran was amazed at the confidence of Dahlin and lowered the sword and placed it back into the trunk and closed its lid.

"I believe you," replied Haran. "I don't know how you will find protection and safety but looking into your eyes I see you have a wisdom beyond me for someone so young."

Haran looked up at the birds, "I apologise for startling you my little friends. I know you will watch over Dahlin most bravely."

Haran went back to his larder and collected some items. "Here, I will give you some food for your journey. You don't know how long it will be before you find something good to eat," he said as he wrapped the food in a cloth.

Haran gave Dahlin the bundle which he placed into his backpack.

"You have been more kind than we deserve," thanked Dahlin. "We will come back to you when our journey takes us this way again."

Haran gave Dahlin a hearty hug and the birds sang a thankful tune.

They turned from Haran and Dahlin walked out of the house while the three little birds led the way. Haran watched them leave and felt a joy within him that he had not felt for many a year. He cried a few gentle tears.

Dahlin and the birds followed the path letting it take them into the direction forward, as forward was the direction on which they knew they had to go. They travelled all day only stopping to take some food and rest their tired limbs for a short while. As the sunlight dimmed and the clouds parted, they could see the half-moon rising and the stars twinkling brighter. They found shelter under a big tree and set up camp for the night and ate some more of Haran's food.

Some distance away Rensin found the house in which Dahlin had discovered the map. He entered the house almost knocking the door from its hinges. He walked into every room; his steps were loud. He kicked the wood from the fire.

"I sense someone has been here," he whispered angrily, "I am not far from the one I seek. I can wait a little longer as I set my trap."

Rensin decided to return to his fortress which was to the north-east slightly away from Dahlin's direction but still not far from the path Dahlin and his companions travelled.

Night had fallen, but Rensin knew his way in the darkness.

Third

Dahlin walked all day following path indicated on the map in a northerly direction towards Hermitage. The birds flew just over his head but occasionally rested on his backpack. The weather had cleared, and the sun was shining, and it grew warmer. His new boots provided protection for his feet against the sharp stones on the path. Every hour or so they rested under a tree and took a little food. They had nearly eaten all the food that Haran had given them, but Dahlin was not worried, he always found something to eat, and the birds discovered much to eat in the trees and on the ground.

By late afternoon they came across a fast-moving though shallow stream. Dahlin was able to replenish his water flask and wash his face and hands. The birds enjoyed a drink and a splash. He saw some fish swimming in the water that he knew were good to eat. Dahlin did not have a fishing line or hook but instead stood very still in the water as the fish swam by his legs. He slowly bent over with his hands just above the water, then as quick as a fly darting away he snatched a fish and threw it onto the bank of the stream. The fish flipped around for a few minutes then stopped.

Dahlin gathered some sticks and branches and built himself a fire within an enclosure of stones. He took his cooking implements from his backpack, scaled the fish, put it in his pan over the flames and let it sizzle and cook until it was ready to be enjoyed.

The three little birds watched all this from a branch above. They were amazed at Dahlin's dexterity and skill in catching the fish. They had never seen anyone like Dahlin.

The sun was setting when the fish was cooked and Dahlin used his fork to break it apart and eat it gratefully. He was thankful for the food that he was given. He gave some little pieces to the birds, and they enjoyed the change in diet as they had never tasted fish.

Dahlin added some more wood to the fire as the air was becoming chilly. He settled down to sleep in the hollow of the tree, thinking over all that had happened and trying to understand where the map was leading him. The little birds took turns keeping watch.

In another part of the forest, Rensin made his way back to his fortress. It was the middle of the night, but Rensin had no trouble finding his way. He noticed a light to his right and decided to see what was there. He discovered a small farm with a stable and a black horse asleep in its pen. He quietly walked to the pen and patted the horse on its neck. He whispered in its ear and the horse awoke, looked directly at Rensin, and nodded its head slowly as if in a daze.

Rensin mounted the horse and led it back to the path. He prodded it into a canter. Riding the horse enabled Rensin to return to his fortress in half the walking time. He arrived at his door just as the sun was rising and tied the horse to a pole near the door. He entered hurriedly and called his servants, the Ravens. Three ravens came immediately from their perches and landed at his feet. They jumped up to his outstretched arms and looked into his eyes.

Rensin ordered them, "I am now sending you on the most important mission. You are to scour from the sky to the northeast of here for a small person dressed in green. Your sharp eyes should be able to discern him from the trees and foliage. Once you have discovered him, return instantly back to me and report on the direction he is headed."

He flung them into the air, and they flew at great speed out of the window.

The sun's rays shone on Dahlin's face, and he was surprised at how long he had slept. He looked up at the three little birds. One was awake and it looked down at him. It then turned to the other two birds and tweeted them awake. They all sang their sunrise song.

After a simple wash in the stream, they ate some breakfast and Dahlin tidied up and removed the campfire so that the surroundings looked undisturbed.

They continued on the path as it led them through more trees and bushes, which thinned out occasionally, and Dahlin could see the sky. Suddenly he saw three dark birds flying overhead. The ravens darted down towards Dahlin and his little birds.

"Quickly!" Dahlin whispered. "Get under cover." Holding their breath they jumped into a bush.

The ravens hovered above the bush, but Dahlin and his companions were well hidden. The ravens croaked at each other then flew off at great speed - back to the fortress of Rensin.

"I fear we may have been seen. All my senses were tingling. My little birds you now need to be more vigilant and scan the sky often. We may be safe for only a little while longer. I sensed a darkness in their purpose." Dahlin sounded concerned.

They continued their way in silence. Dahlin's thoughts asked him many questions. Is there an answer to my quest? Am I to be a wanderer of this dream? Is it a dream? Is it a search for my losses and a solution for them? Will I find someone to give me comfort and insight into my troubles? Dahlin pondered all these questions for many hours as they walked. Unbeknown to the travellers, the path now led them closer to Rensin's fortress which was not marked on the map.

The ravens swiftly flew into Rensin's fortress window and Rensin deciphered their cawing. He now knew where his adversary would be in a couple of days. Closer than he expected and close to being within his grasp. He decided he did not wish to harm this person yet. Rensin wanted to find out what it was that took this person on the path and where he was headed. Perhaps he could discover the purpose of the search and determine if it held any value, whether it's treasure or valuable information. Rensin was a person who was selfish for whatever benefited him and added to his power. A power that gave him domination over others.

Rensin walked over to his large wardrobe and pulled out old clothing, including a cloak and a hat. He looked at them and thought, "These will cover me and hide my intentions. I will lure him into my fortress and through my piteous behaviour find out his purpose and take it from him." Rensin smiled cruelly and his ravens cackled their approval.

"Fly into the sky once again my dark pets and get another bearing on his position. I think it will be soon that I will have him in my grasp," Rensin laughed.

Dahlin and his birds trekked stealthily all day. They found another hollow in a tree and decided to set up camp nearby. Night had fallen, but Dahlin was able to gather enough wood and quickly got a fire blazing to warm them and keep away any night animals. So far on their journey, they had not encountered any dangerous animals. They had seen deer, rabbits and wildfowl. These animals had not run away when Dahlin approached but gave curious looks as if a friend had walked by. Many birds flew overhead and looked down on them. It was only the ravens that troubled Dahlin. He had not seen them again but that did not mean they would not come again.

Dahlin was still wary, as occasionally during the night he heard the howling of wolves. Were they friends or were they foes?

After their simple meal of seeds and berries, Dahlin wrapped himself in his blanket and huddled in the hollow of the tree. The little birds perched on a branch just above Dahlin to take turns keeping sentry.

After an hour the fire burned low. The birds saw this and two of them dropped to the ground and attempted to pick up a branch to put it on the fire. They heard a noise and to their horror two red eyes looked at them only a short distance away. It was a wolf!

The wolf entered the campsite, and the birds chirped loudly and flew towards Dahlin. They could not wake him. The wolf walked slowly towards Dahlin. They were prepared to attack the wolf to protect Dahlin. The birds flew towards the wolf, but they quickly stopped, not believing what they saw.

The wolf lay down close to Dahlin, just outside the entrance to the hollow and looked up at the birds. It then looked at Dahlin and gave a contented sound. Closed its eyes and fell asleep.

The birds looked at each other in amazement. They chirped to each other happy that all was now safe. They flew back up to the branch above Dahlin and kept turns watching during the night. All was quiet except for the gentle snoring of the wolf.

The next morning the air was chilly, and the fire had gone out. The birds wished they were strong enough to carry wood and start a fire. As they looked down at the ashes, they saw the wolf awake. He sniffed the fire and ran into the bushes. He returned shortly carrying twigs in his mouth and dropped them on the ashes. He then put a stone beneath the twigs and scratched it with his claws. A spark flew out into the twigs, and they caught alight. He ran back into the bushes and came back with a few larger branches and dropped them onto the flames. The fire built up strength. Again, the wolf darted away and returned quickly dragging a larger log and swinging it around into the air it fell onto the flames. The campfire now blazed and warmed all around.

Dahlin stirred and opened his eyes and was greeted by the birds. They all chirped loudly trying to tell him about the fire. Dahlin looked over to the campfire and saw its flames warming away the cold air. He looked back at the birds.

"Who started the fire? Was it you?" he inquired.

They turned to point at the wolf. It was gone.

"You are getting very clever, my little friends."

The birds looked at each other and just shrugged their wings.

Dahlin studied the map and decided to follow the path that led northeast as it seemed to be an easier way around to get to the mountain of Hermitage. Little did he know that it would lead him closer to Rensin's fortress.

After some breakfast they set out again following the path. The trees covered most of the sky from their view but every now and then the sky appeared. When it did the ravens, who were circling above, saw where they were headed and darted back to Rensin before being noticed. One of the little birds thought it saw a dark spot in the sky and it shuddered. The others had not noticed.

The ravens reported back to Rensin who was pleased with the news. He dressed in the old clothes and covered his head with a hooded cloak. He walked at a quick pace and intended to meet Dahlin at the big rock which was near the path Dahlin would pass.

After an hour Rensin reached the big rock and decided to wait. He sat at the base of the rock and pretended to be resting.

Dahlin and his birds stayed on the path as it turned north and saw a big rock not far ahead. It looked like someone was sitting on the ground by the rock dressed in old clothes—perhaps a stranger or danger. Dahlin sensed an unease that warned him to be on his guard. They approached cautiously.

As they neared, Rensin looked up and greeted them with a smile. He had roughened up his face so that it looked old and worn.

"Ah, travellers." he said. "I am so lucky that you have come this way as I need help. I must get back to my dwelling before nightfall. I grew very tired and was afraid I wouldn't make it. Do you mind helping an old man safely back to his home, and I will prepare a meal in thanks? You may stay and rest before you continue your journey tomorrow."

Dahlin felt unsure but also felt he could not abandon someone in need. He looked at his birds who chirped worriedly.

"Yes, we will help you. Here take my arm and let me help you get to your feet," said Dahlin.

He held out his arm and Rensin pretended to struggle as he rose to his feet. The strength of Rensin's hand on his arm did not reassure Dahlin that this was an old man.

"Where is your dwelling?" asked Dahlin.

"Not far. We follow the path for a while then turn on another narrower path that leads east. My dwelling is in that direction. Not far, not far," Rensin pointed and thought to himself, "This is too easy!"

They set off but could only walk at the speed of Rensin who, bent over, pretended to walk slowly and with a limp.

"You need a walking stick," suggested Dahlin.

"I did have one, but it broke along my way," lied Rensin.

They walked for about ten minutes then Rensin asked Dahlin.

"I don't often see people on this path, is there a reason for you being in this forest?"

"We are just taking a long trek to enjoy the countryside and to see what is in this part of our country," Dahlin carefully replied without lying.

"We?" queried Rensin.

"I have been accompanied by my new friends, the three little birds. They have kept with me most of the way. I guess it's because I feed them special treats," Dahlin laughed a little in embarrassment realising his mistake in mentioning the birds.

"Really? I thought birds could find food themselves," answered Rensin.

"Oh, they keep me company and I enjoy not feeling alone in this forest. Speaking of the forest," attempting to change the conversation, Dahlin asked, "Does it have a name?"

Dahlin did not want Rensin to know of the map in his backpack that called the forest, *Mountain Wood*.

"It is called *Mountain Wood*, and has had that name for a long time," Rensin replied truthfully.

Dahlin felt the truth was spoken but sensed that Rensin was devious and decided to be careful.

"An interesting name. Do you know why it is called *Mountain Wood*?" asked Dahlin.

"I am not sure, perhaps it has something to do with the forest being below that mountain." Rensin pointed in the direction of Hermitage.

"Is there something special up there?" Dahlin questioned further.

"Not as far as I know," replied Rensin.

Dahlin felt this was true and was pleased that Rensin did not know about Hermitage.

"You look like you have lived here in these woods for some time. Surely you explored the mountain and its surroundings in the past?" questioned Dahlin, as he wanted to be sure Rensin knew nothing about Hermitage.

"I may look old, but I have not lived in these parts for long, perhaps five years. I lived further south for most of my life, once in the town of Sunatin. Have you been there?" inquired Rensin.

"I have been to a few towns, it is possible. I don't always remember every town's name. I don't stay long in one place." Dahlin replied truthfully without giving away more information.

He sensed a cunning curiousity in Rensin's question and felt he did not want to tell him that he had stayed with Johan, the carpenter. Dahlin was unaware that the 'old man' was the son of Johan. Neither had told each other their names and Dahlin felt that perhaps he should tell Rensin, it might reveal more to his feelings.

"I am sorry, but I have been neglectful in introducing myself. My name is Dahlin." As he spoke, he noticed a spark of satisfaction on Rensin's face.

Dahlin felt the reason would soon be discovered. Rensin smiled and kept walking but did not immediately reply. Dahlin sensed a discontent and felt more wary of this strange man. The birds twittered above keeping their distance.

"I feel tired and want to focus my energy on reaching my dwelling. There we may relax and talk more after our meal," stated Rensin finally.

Dahlin felt relieved as he did not like talking to to this 'old man' at all.

Soon they reached the narrower path that led to Rensin's fortress. It grew darker as evening gathered around them. Rensin quickened his pace and no longer limped.

Dahlin saw this and asked, "You have lost your

limp and your slowness, are you feeling better?"

"Er, yes, yes. I get excited when I am near my dwelling, and it gives me extra energy," Rensin gave as an excuse and hurried on.

Dahlin and the birds followed just a few steps behind him.

In front of them appeared Rensin's fortress, a large two-storied dark building with several windows and two chimneys. The front door was huge and looked heavy. Rensin drew out his key and opened the door, it creaked a welcome.

Dahlin entered but the birds flew to an open window and perched on its sill. They did not want to enter.

"When you said a dwelling, I thought it would be a small hut. This place is huge," Dahlin stated plainly.

Rensin looked back at Dahlin. "It is just my dwelling. I have added to it over time as my interests grew."

Dahlin did not ask, but wondered what the 'interests' might be, though he sensed they were probably not good.

Fourth

Rensin, in his disguise as an old man, showed Dahlin around some of the rooms in the fortress. They passed some stairs leading down..

"What is down there?" asked Dahlin.

"It is just a storeroom, for things that I wish to keep cool," lied Rensin.

"Such as?" queried Dahlin.

"Wine, cheese and eggs. Some other things." Rensin lied again.

They went back into the room with the fire. The little birds chirped from the window when they saw Dahlin again, they had been worried because they did not want to enter the room.

"You have been carrying your backpack all day and you still have it on your back. Take it off and place it on the chair over there," suggested Rensin as he prepared a couple of bowls of vegetable soup.

"Oh yes, that is true. I get so used to it that I am not aware I'm still carrying it," replied Dahlin.

Dahlin took his backpack from his back and placed it on a chair which was not far from the fire.

While Dahlin had his back turned, Rensin sprinkled some powder into the bowl of soup he had prepared for Dahlin. The little birds noticed this and started chirping. Rensin looked at them fiercely and they stopped.

Dahlin turned to see the little birds nodding their heads at each other and towards him. He became wary.

They sat at the table and Rensin talked about things he had seen in the forest pretending he enjoyed flowers, insects and animals. He took his spoon and drank some of the soup.

"Ah, this is delicious. Try some, you will find it very refreshing," he urged Dahlin.

Dahlin took some of the vegetable soup onto his spoon and moved it to his mouth. Rensin watched intently. As the soup entered Dahlin's mouth, he sensed danger and only swallowed a drop or two. Immediately he knew something was wrong and dropped the spoon. It fell to the floor and Rensin watched it clatter and spill its contents. Dahlin spat out what was in his mouth, but the poison was strong, and he collapsed unconscious to the floor.

Rensin rose with a flourish, threw off the old man's clothes and walked steadily towards Dahlin's body. He harshly grabbed Dahlin's arms and dragged him out of the room. He went down the stairs and threw Dahlin into his dark and dirty dungeon. He slammed the door shut and locked it with the key that hung on a hook opposite the door. He laughed as he looked at the unconscious body through the small hole in the door. He stayed there a few minutes thinking about what to do next to rid himself of this hindrance to his life.

Meanwhile, upstairs the three little birds were in shock. They flew into the room trying to see where Rensin had taken Dahlin. They heard the dungeon door slam and feared it was too dangerous to go down the stairs while Rensin was there outside the door. They looked up and saw the ceiling beams and decided to hide out of sight until he left. It was just in time, as Rensin swung around and stamped up the stairs not noticing the birds above his head.

The three little birds flew down to the hole in the door and perched there for a moment watching Dahlin. To their great delight, he started to groan and move then sat up holding his head. They flew in and rested on his shoulders chirping quietly.

"I knew there was something amiss when I raised the spoon to my mouth. It must have been a very strong potion as I only swallowed a drop. If I had taken a mouth full, I would still be unconscious for many hours." Dahlin took his little frightened friends in his hands and comforted them by patting them gently.

Dahlin walked slowly over to the door and looked through the hole. He could see the key on the hook opposite.

"If only we could get the key," he said quietly.

Two of the little birds heard this and darted out of the hole and over to the hook. They both lifted the key off the hook in their beaks.

It was heavy and it fell from their beaks and clattered to the floor. They froze and listened. Rensin was busy getting wood for the fire and did not hear the noise. Two ravens were outside of the fortress but one was in the room.

The birds picked up the key and flew it over to Dahlin. He took the key and looked for the keyhole on his side of the door, but it was missing.

"Well, I guess that's a good idea, not having a keyhole on the prisoner's side," he laughed a little. He looked at the birds.

"Do you think you would be able to put the key in the lock and then turn it?"

The birds looked at each other and took deep breaths. One of them put the key in its beak and hovered over the keyhole trying to get the key in. The others helped by holding it straight, lining it up and moving it into the hole. Their wings fluttered furiously as they had never attempted anything like this before.

Dahlin watched the birds' effort and smiled when they succeeded putting it into the keyhole.

"Now you just have to turn it," he said hopefully.

The birds dropped to the ground for a little rest for they knew that to turn the key would take all their strength. They looked at each other and twittered instructions waving their wings around.

The three little birds took different parts of the key in their beaks. They flew as hard as they could in the same direction, but nothing happened, the key did not move. They dropped to the floor exhausted.

"Perhaps, my little friends, you turn the key the other way," suggested Dahlin.

They looked at each other and nodded their heads as if to say, "Of course!"

They each took a deep breath and flew back up to the key. Taking a different part in their beaks. They flew, in the other direction, as hard as they could. The key moved. Encouraged by this they tried harder, flapping their wings in unison. The key moved some more and finally clicked. Dahlin pushed the door, and it opened. They all gave a quiet cheer.

Suddenly a raven dived in swiftly and mercilessly attacked the birds. They flew up trying to get away but were exhausted from their effort to open the door. The raven, seeing their tiredness, made a laughing sound. This was its mistake. Dahlin heard the noise and swung the door around to see but it hit the raven knocking it to the ground. It lay still breathing shallowly. Dahlin gasped seeing what had happened. He approached the raven and picked it up gently and put it on the floor of the prison. He gave it a caring gaze then closed and locked the door. The raven was too big to get out through the hole in the door. They all looked down at the raven.

"I pity it. I hope one day it will get away from Rensin and be free," said Dahlin sadly.

The little birds gave Dahlin a quizzical look.

"You looked puzzled? Don't you know that I care for creatures, good or bad?"

They chirped a question, which Dahlin was able to interpret.

"Yes, you're right. I know his name is Rensin. He is Johan's wayward son. Let's go quietly up the stairs and see what he's up to. I'm surprised he hasn't heard all the noise we've been making." The little birds perched on Dahlin's shoulders as he went towards the stairs.

Meanwhile upstairs, Rensin thought Dahlin would be unconscious for hours, so he finished his soup and ate some bread. He leant back in his chair and laughed maliciously. He looked over to the window and noticed the birds were gone and wondered where they were hiding. Perhaps his ravens could find them and have some fun. Ravens liked teasing little birds.

He got up from his chair and looked outside

from the door. He opened the door a little wider and his three ravens flew in.

"Have you seen Dahlin's little friends?"

They indicated that they had not.

"Then fly around and see if you can find them. One of you go down to the dungeon. The other two fly around outside. If you find them bring them back here."

The ravens departed. Rensin went outside to get some more wood for the fire. While he was gone the one raven left in the room heard a noise from the dungeon. It flew down the stairs to investigate. Little did it realise that soon it would be imprisoned.

Rensin re-entered the room and threw the wood onto the fire, making it blaze as if in fury. He went over and picked up Dahlin's backpack and hurriedly took everything out. He stopped when he saw the map.

"This should prove interesting," he said to himself.

He spread it out onto the table and examined it closely. Rensin had a good memory, so he intended to memorise the map and then destroy it. Though he had been in the area for a few years, there was much of the land he did not know about. He had kept to himself in his fortress wallowing in his anger and resentment. He only ventured out to steal for his supplies. It was only in the last few months that he sensed the presence of Dahlin in the area. He felt purity and goodness, and he detested it. He wanted to destroy it. He had been deprived of the things he wanted to do by his father who had stopped him. He could not endure his father's advice. He wanted to do what he wanted to do. No one was going to tell him otherwise - especially his father.

Dahlin silently walked up the stairs with the birds on his shoulders. He carefully looked into the room and saw Rensin studying the map. He watched him for a few minutes. Two ravens flew in through the window and perched near the table. Suddenly Rensin crushed the map in his hands and threw it into the fire.

Quick as a flash one of the birds darted for the map and plucked it out of the fire before the flames could take hold. He flew back to Dahlin who quickly folded the map and put it into his pocket. One of the ravens swooped down onto the bird sending it hurtling across the room. It hit a wall and fell to the floor. Dahlin looked shocked at his little friend on the floor, not moving.

The other two birds flew up and pecked at the ravens who cawed a laugh and went for the birds at great speed. They all flew around and around the room pecking and clawing at each other.

While this happened, Dahlin and Rensin stared at each other. Rensin looked surprised.

"I thought you would still be unconscious. Perhaps there is more strength in you than I presumed," laughed Rensin. He picked up a log near the fireplace, waved it around and started towards Dahlin.

Dahlin quickly turned and ran down the stairs. He found a dark corner in which he crouched low and blended into the darkness. He felt a strange sensation come over him, deadening all his emotions.

Rensin, in fury, rushed down the stairs, stopped by the prison door and saw through the door hole one of his ravens on the floor. He then walked slowly in Dahlin's direction but could not see nor sense him in the dark.

"I will get a light and find you very quickly," threatened Rensin. "There is no other way out except by the stairs."

Rensin turned and walked back to the prison door and, as the key was still in the lock, turned it and went in to see if his raven was dead or alive. He bent over and picked the bird up roughly and it opened its eyes. It stared at Rensin with a strange look. Rensin was baffled by it.

Suddenly the door banged shut and the key turned. Rensin looked up to see Dahlin's face at the door-hole.

"I will take my departure now, Rensin," Dahlin said calmly, "but I will leave the key in the door. I feel sure that your ravens know how to turn it to unlock the door. My little birds were able to do so." With that, he turned and went upstairs.

"I will find you!" called out Rensin in anger.

Dahlin entered the upstairs room to see the two ravens and his two little birds flying around in circles pecking at each other. He looked to see whether his third bird was still on the floor. It had struggled to its feet and looked very poorly. He rushed over, picked it up and put it into his shirt pocket to keep it safe. His backpack was on the floor with its contents scattered about. He swiftly gathered everything back into his pack and swung it onto his back. He paused and thought for the briefest moment.

He ran outside and closed the door behind him. He went to the open window and called his birds. They saw him and flew at their top speed out of the window. Dahlin quickly closed the shutters trapping the ravens. He looked at his friends and urgently said:

"That was very exciting but let us quickly depart away from here. Rensin will soon be freed."

It was after midnight and still very dark. Dahlin had excellent night sight and speedily led his friends, who perched on his shoulders, away from the fortress. The night sky was filled with stars and Dahlin felt they twinkled delightfully at their escape from the treachery of Rensin.

They picked their way through the bushes not wanting to use the narrow path that had led them to the fortress. Dahlin had a good sense of direction, and they soon reached the wider path, but he kept to its edges to prevent leaving a trail of his footsteps.

Dahlin maintained his consistent pace for over an hour but grew tired. He risked stopping for a few moments and took a drink from his flask. He offered it to his bird friends. They thanked him with a little chirp. He took the injured bird from his pocket and gave it a drink. It looked up at him and gave a feeble chirp to reassure him that it felt better.

"My little friends now that you have saved me and risked your lives to protect me, I would be honoured if you would allow me to give you names."

The three little birds chirped in unison and gave their approval.

Dahlin thought and walked on quickly as he wished to get further away from danger. He looked at each bird and tried to find a name that described their personalities and strengths.

He looked at the injured bird in his pocket. "Without thinking of yourself and the danger you faced, you saved the map. I would like to give you the name, Intrepidus which means fearless."

The little bird tweeted his acceptance of being called Intrepidus. The other two birds eagerly waited for their names to be given. One was on Dahlin's right shoulder, the other on his left.

Dahlin looked at the one on his right shoulder. "You have been watchful and aware of the things around us. Would you accept the name Vigilans, which means to be vigilant?"

The little bird jumped for joy and tweeted his

acceptance to be called Vigilans.

Dahlin looked at the little bird on his left shoulder. "I am sorry to name you last but you have never felt afraid of anything, even being named last," laughed Dahlin. "Would you accept the name, Animo, which means courage?"

The little bird waved its wings, spun around in a circle, and landed back on Dahlin's shoulder, happy to be called Animo.

Dahlin continued walking at a fast pace for several hours, carrying his very happy birds who were delighted with their new names. They tweeted and chirped quietly, rejoicing at becoming a family with Dahlin as their guardian. They resolved amongst themselves to be loyal and to defend Dahlin with their lives if it ever came to that choice. Dahlin had found companions worthy of his journey. He was pleased that he was no longer alone.

As dawn came, while they sang their joyful tune to the rising sun, they found the stream named *The Winding Water,* according to the map. Here they refreshed themselves and washed away the dirt of Rensin's fortress. They felt restored.

Dahlin and the birds found nuts and berries to satisfy their hunger. Dahlin stored enough food for a couple of days in his backpack. He never took more than he needed for two reasons, one, because there may be others in search of food, and he did not want to deprive them of nourishment. Two, it would make his backpack too heavy. He laughed to himself at that thought!

Meanwhile, after Dahlin's escape, Rensin sat on the floor of his dungeon thinking of what to do next to catch Dahlin. His two other ravens looked through the door hole wondering what he was doing and why he did not want to be released.

Finally, Rensin looked up at the ravens and firmly said, "Turn the key and let me out of here!"

They immediately obeyed. Their beaks were strong, and they easily turned the key. Rensin thundered through them as they scattered out of his way and went upstairs. He left the injured raven on the floor of the prison. Rensin stormed up the stairs and threw open the window and peered outside into the darkness and clenched his teeth in anger. It was after midnight, and he realised he could do nothing until morning. He went over to the stove.

The two ravens flew to their companion and helped it to its feet. It gave them a strange look and they fell back in shock for they knew what it meant. It would no longer obey Rensin. They all flew up into the room where Rensin was making himself some food to eat. The two ravens were cawing at Rensin. He looked up and saw the injured raven fly out of the window.

"Good riddance," said Rensin. "An injured bird is of no use to me."

Little did he know where the raven was headed.

Fifth

Rensin looked at his remaining two ravens.

"Are you going to be cowards too and fly away like your pathetic brother?"

The two ravens shook their heads and voiced with their guttural speech that they would be loyal to Rensin to the very end.

"The very end!" Rensin laughed. "The only end I desire is to defeat Dahlin. And that is what I will do. Go out and find him while I get some sleep. The darkness will hide you from their eyes."

The ravens flew out into the night.

Rensin ate much food which fuelled his anger.

He went up to his bedroom and tried to sleep. He awoke many times during the night, which only increased his rage.

In contrast to Rensin, Dahlin had a peaceful sleep. He decided to rest during the mid-morning and hide from the ravens in case they appeared. He and his birds had gone off the path and found a small cave covered by overhanging branches. Dahlin hid inside, and using his backpack as a pillow, was soon asleep. His birds, Animo, Intrepidus and Vigilans, watched in the branches above, taking turns to be on alert for any sign of Rensin's dangerous ravens.

Dahlin slept for a couple of hours but was awakened when his birds flew down and warned him that they saw two ravens flying above.

"We are well hidden, so they probably didn't see us. I wonder why there are only two ravens. What happened to the one that attacked us in the dungeon?" pondered Dahlin.

He also thought about Rensin's anger. "Why does he have such anger in him against everyone? And he seems to dislike me terribly that he wanted to trick me, then poison me. I am blessed that my little friends protected me and for an intuitiveness within me that warned me of danger. I have noticed the feeling growing stronger within me over the last few months as I have set out on my journey. I need someone to talk to about it, perhaps there will be someone at Hermitage. I have a feeling there will be, but we are still far away. If we find another dwelling on this path, we will ask if we can rest for a few days." Dahlin thought over all these matters as they followed the path. Fortunately, there was no sign of the ravens in the sky.

After a couple of hours, Dahlin checked the map and decided to keep following the path as it kept to the forest, and the overhanging branches hid them from the prying eyes of the patrolling ravens. Every now and then the trees parted, and they went quickly through long grass over the small hills. The weather was now sunny, so it kept them warm, and the scenery lifted their spirits.

They came to a part of the path where it widened and they noticed the tracks of wheels, probably from a cart. The trees thinned and the path undulated, and they saw that the tracks of the cart went off the path to the left and over a hill. Dahlin thought this would be interesting to see where it led, so they followed the tracks and once over the hill saw a farmhouse only two hundred steps away. Dahlin felt he needed to rest for a few days, so decided to visit the farmhouse in the hope the farmer would give him work.

The little birds flew from Dahlin's shoulder up higher out of the way into a tree not far from the house. Dahlin entered the yard of the farm and noticed several horses in the fenced yard outside their stable. There was also a chestnut stallion in a yard by itself. It ran around furiously shaking its head and neighed loudly.

Dahlin was curious and walked over to the stallion. It stopped in the middle of its yard and stared at Dahlin for several moments. It turned and shook its head. It gave a little squeal and trotted over to Dahlin who had rested his arms on the fence. As it approached, Dahlin put out his hand and patted it on the nose and neck. The horse sighed and relaxed, then nuzzled into Dahlin's chest.

"Hey, what are you doing?" An angry voice shouted from behind Dahlin. He turned to see a big set man stomping towards him. It was the farmer, and he did not sound pleased.

Dahlin turned towards the farmer and smiled.

"I was just curious why the horse was by itself. I am sorry if I have done anything wrong," apologised Dahlin.

"Who are you and what do you want? I don't like strangers, especially those who mess with my horses," replied the farmer gruffly.

"My name is Dahlin, and I am a traveller. I need to rest for a little time and would like to offer you my services in exchange for a place to sleep. I am quite good at repairing wooden things. I spent two weeks working for a carpenter in Sunatan, and he was pleased with my efforts. Would you be able to let me work for you?"

"Huh, that was probably Johan, what would he know? I do need some fences fixed around the stable. I don't want my horses escaping as I need them to pull my wagon and to plough my fields."

The farmer looked at the chestnut stallion. "I am puzzled that this horse didn't bite your hand off. I am going to sell it as it won't do anything I want it to. It has kicked me several times."

The horse snorted when it looked at the farmer then put its head over the fence and touched Dahlin's back. Dahlin turned and gently patted it.

"Get away from that horse!" roared the farmer.

"Does the horse have a name?" inquired Dahlin, ignoring the farmer's outburst.

"No, of course not, it's a wild one. I am selling

it," replied the farmer. "My name is Sevel. You can work for me for a few days to get the fences fixed and you can sleep in the stables, but you will have to find your own food. I don't want you in my house."

"I thank you. I think I will sleep in the stable of this stallion," said Dahlin as he looked the farmer in the eyes.

"Well, don't blame me if he stomps all over you," stammered Sevel.

Evening had come and the light was fading. The farmer walked back to his house and slammed the door. Dahlin heard him talking to someone and wondered if it was his wife.

Dahlin turned and jumped the fence into the yard of the stallion, who immediately came over and Dahlin patted him on the neck and talked to him softly. The horse sighed, then suddenly snorted in the direction of the house. Dahlin looked around and saw a woman walking quickly towards them.

"I'm Karlene, the farmer's wife. He told me about you, and I wanted to make sure you were not a thief. And ..." she stopped speaking and muttered to herself. She could not believe that Dahlin was in the horse yard with the wild stallion.

Dahlin looked at her and smiled. "He seems quite content with me."

She stood frozen on the spot for several moments, and her stern face melted into a gentle smile.

"I, er," she tried to say something but was taken aback by her change in mood. "Have you had anything to eat?" she finally asked.

"Sevel said I could sleep in the stable, but I had to find my own food. There are plenty of wild fruits around that I will collect shortly," he replied.

"Oh no. Don't take any notice of Sevel. He has been very upset and moody for some time due to our crops failing. He hasn't given me a smile for ages. If only our crops would grow. Let's not talk about that. Stay where you are. I will be back shortly." She hurried back to the house.

Dahlin continued patting the horse and talking to it softly. Animo, Intrepidus and Vigilans had been watching everything from the branch above the horse yard. They flew down and perched on Dahlin's shoulders and sang a song to the horse. He shook his head pleased at their song. They flew over and landed on his back and nested by closing their eyes.

Dahlin heard the house door shut and saw Karlene approaching with a bundle in her arms.

"Here you are, a loaf of fresh bread and a pot of honey," she said gently as she handed over the food to Dahlin.

The bread was wrapped in a clean cloth and was still warm. The honey was in a little pot.

"You can keep the pot of honey in your backpack, it won't spill, the lid is tight," she informed him in a motherly tone.

"You have been more gracious than I deserve," said Dahlin. "I haven't done any work yet." He laughed, giving her another smile.

"Yes, you have. You have tamed that wild beast of a horse," she giggled and turned and almost skipped joyfully back to the house.

It was getting dark and chilly, so Dahlin led the horse into its stable and covered it with its blanket. He gave it some hay and filled the water trough. The little birds flew up into the stable rafters and closed their eyes for they were very tired. They felt safe.

Dahlin gathered some hay and made himself a place to sleep. He took his blanket from his backpack and placed it over the hay. He sat down and closed his eyes and said a prayer of thanks. He ate some bread and honey and looked around the stable. The stallion was asleep, as were his little bird friends. He used his backpack as a pillow, covered himself in his blanket, and he too was fast asleep in a minute.

The next day the farmer Sevel barked orders at Dahlin and showed him the damaged fences.

"I can fix those easily," said Dahlin cheerfully. "Where are the tools?" he asked Sevel.

Sevel glared at him and said, "Over there in that shed. Take your cheerful little self over there and find them. I've got other things to do." He turned and stormed off.

Dahlin watched him go and sighed. "Some people are never happy," he thought to himself.

The shed was a mess with tools and implements in disarray. He decided to tidy it up before he tackled the fences. He found what he needed, a hammer, saw and nails and walked back to the fence. There were some planks of wood lying around so he gathered up those that were suitable.

"Why are you taking so long?" yelled Sevel from a distance, unaware that his shed was now tidy.

Dahlin was going to explain but decided he did not want to yell back at Sevel.

"Don't worry. I will have them mended shortly," he said loud enough for Sevel to hear.

"It'd better be done properly," Sevel yelled back as he walked over the hill to one of his paddocks.

It took Dahlin a few hours to mend the fence. He had to saw new lengths from the planks, remove the damaged palings and nail the new ones in place. By mid-afternoon he was finished, and he stood up to look at his work. Suddenly he was startled by a voice behind.

"You think that's good enough. Proud of yourself, are you?" snarled Sevel from behind him.

Dahlin turned to face him and said, "If it is not good enough, I will do it again. How would you like it?"

Sevel was going to say something but when he looked at the fence, he knew it could not be done better.

"It'll do," he uttered and walked away.

Dahlin just shook his head. He gathered all the tools and took them back to the shed. As he walked towards the stable, Karlene called out to him while she hurried towards him, holding a flask in her hand.

Dahlin greeted her with a smile. "You look very fresh today," he said.

She was a little embarrassed and giggled.

"Here have a drink. I don't think you have stopped all day. Well, the fence looks wonderful. You have done a good job. Was Sevel pleased?" she asked.

Dahlin scratched his head. "That was hard to judge. I guess so," replied Dahlin.

"Hmm, he rarely gives praise. What do you plan to do now?" she inquired.

"I need to continue my travels. I will sleep in the stable one more night and start early in the morning. I will give you my farewells now and thank you for your kind hospitality," responded Dahlin.

That night after Dahlin had seen to the needs of the chestnut stallion and was settling down on his straw bed he heard a noise outside the stable. He went to investigate. He opened the stable door and startled Karlene who was placing a bag on a hook near the door.

"Oh, I thought you were asleep," she said. "I knew you were leaving early so I wanted to make sure you had food for your journey. I have a newly baked loaf of bread; some fruit and another pot of honey. Do you have enough water?" she asked.

"You are extremely kind, and I appreciate your gifts. They will sustain me for several days. And yes, I do have some water. I have already filled my flask," he said softly.

"That is wonderful," she said. She stood there for some moments hesitating as if she wanted to do something else. Then quickly she gave Dahlin a big hug, sniffled a little and walked back to her house without looking back.

Dahlin smiled and watched her, "Thank you," he said, but wasn't sure if she heard him. She did, and smiled and sniffled as she entered her house.

Dahlin could hear Sevel say, "What's the matter

with you?" She did not reply.

Dahlin went to his bed and Animo, Intrepidus and Vigilans flew down and rested on his chest as it rose and fell when he breathed. He looked at them.

"My little friends, people can surprise us sometimes. And the surprises can be delightful. We must always believe that our actions can bring happiness to others, and in turn, that happiness will come back to us. It is an endless cycle of treasures."

The little birds tweeted to each other that they agreed. They all went to their places of rest and quickly fell asleep.

Early in the morning, before sunrise, Dahlin got up and had a little breakfast. He patted the chestnut stallion and whispered in its ear a goodbye. The horse gave a little sigh and groan as if to indicate that he was sad that Dahlin was leaving.

The little birds flew down from their perch in the stable and landed on Dahlin's shoulders. He opened the stable door quietly, not wanting to make Sevel aware that he was departing.

He quickly walked over the hill and found the path in the trees which led him in a north-westerly direction – towards Hermitage, though that was still a long distance away.

Dahlin walked at a steady pace for several hours. The little birds flew above looking out for any dangers. Occasionally, he could hear rustling in the trees above. But when he looked up, he could not see what was making the noise. The little birds saw nothing, too.

They had not seen or encountered the *Winding Water* stream again but according to the map it would cross their path soon and would be wider, like a river. Dahlin hoped there was a bridge as he did not want to wade through cold and deep water. Also, Dahlin wanted to catch a fish to give him more sustenance in addition to the food Karlene had provided. The birds were unaffected by these worries as they readily discovered food and could fly over the stream effortlessly. They wished they were strong enough to carry Dahlin, but they knew he was too heavy.

Dahlin looked at the map and realised they would soon have to cross the *Winding Water*. He could hear the waters as they walked out of the trees. The stream was now a river. It would take at least thirty or more of Dahlin's steps to cross, and it was flowing rapidly. It looked deep, probably over Dahlin's head. But only ten steps to their right he saw the bridge. It was a suspended log rope bridge. The ropes stretched from tree to tree either side of the water. The logs looked old, and some were broken with gaps not wider than Dahlin's step. There were two rope handrails on either side to help with balancing, but it still looked precarious.

As he walked towards the bridge, he heard the sound of a horse galloping at great speed. His normal calmness left him, and he felt it must be Rensin who he knew had a horse.

Dahlin ran towards the bridge and stepped on the first log, it broke under his foot. He tried the second one and it held his weight. He looked around but could not see the horse or rider. He knew he must not rush, as every part of the bridge looked like it would collapse if he put it under stress.

He took more steps and reached the middle of the bridge. He stopped to gather his breath, and the bridge started to sway. The little birds were hovering just above his head. They looked anxiously at each other, not knowing what to do if Dahlin fell.

Suddenly there was a cracking sound. The ropes at either end of the bridge started to unravel. Several log steps broke and fell into the fast-flowing waters.

Dahlin knew he had to get across quickly. He stepped onto the logs as lightly as he could. After a few steps the ropes gave way. and the bridge swung to the left. The little birds, in desperation, dived down and grabbed the straps of Dahlin's backpack in their feet and lifted him up. They were not strong enough. The bridge vanished into the frothing waves. Dahlin felt himself falling.

Suddenly from the trees shot a black blur. It dived towards Dahlin. It was the raven! The little birds saw it coming and were afraid it would strike Dahlin and send him into the river to be swept downstream.

To their utter amazement, it grabbed the backpack straps in its feet and lifted Dahlin into the air above the river's waves. The little birds knew it could not lift Dahlin alone, so they doubled their efforts. Their wings flapping furiously as they all carried Dahlin across to the other side, where they dropped onto the sandy bank, exhausted.

They sat there for several minutes, not speaking, and tried to catch their breaths.

The raven was panting a few steps away from Dahlin, who looked at it and reached out his hand towards it.

"Come here my new friend," he said gently.

The raven walked slowly towards Dahlin. The three little birds watched in alarm.

Dahlin saw this and said, "Don't worry, my little

friends. I think we may have a new companion."

The raven reached Dahlin who took it in his hands and patted it.

"I am very fortunate that you came just in time to assist my friends and rescued me. I am very happy and thank you for your help," said Dahlin.

The raven bowed its head in acknowledgment. It looked into Dahlin's eyes and shed a tear as its way of saying sorry for what it had done under Rensin's commands.

"I forgive you and will no longer think of it," whispered Dahlin. "And to make this reconciliation special, would you mind if I gave you the name of Felix – which means fortunate and happy?"

The raven bowed its head and looked up into Dahlin's eyes. It made a soft warbling sound which expressed its acceptance and happiness to now be amongst new and true friends.

Dahlin heard a neighing sound and realised that Rensin may be nearby. In the excitement of the river crossing, and being saved by Felix, he had momentarily forgotten. He looked over the river and saw a horse jump through the bushes on the other side. It reared up onto its hind legs and neighed loudly.

There was no rider on its back.

Sixth

Dahlin gazed in amazement. It was the chestnut stallion from Sevel's farm! He had escaped and followed them. He jumped into the water and with its great strength swam across the river. When he reached the sandy bank, he shook himself vigorously. The water spray reached Dahlin, who rose to his feet and walked over to the horse and hugged it, whispering gentle words into its ear.

"You have been seeking us, and now you have found us."

The stallion nodded its head and stomped its feet in joy.

Dahlin wrapped his hands around the horse's neck and looked directly into its eyes.

"Would you allow me to give you the name of Quaesitor, which means a seeker?" asked Dahlin.

The chestnut stallion gave a blowing sound and nodded its head, which indicated his approval and acceptance.

Dahlin looked around. He saw Animo, Intrepidus, Vigilans, and Felix, his bird companions. Now he had Quaesitor. A family of friends. He knew they would accompany him devotedly on his journey to Hermitage. They would protect and support him.

Quaesitor neighed and turned its head to its back and knelt on its forelegs. He was telling Dahlin that it was alright for him to be carried on its back. Dahlin was pleased; for now his travelling would be quicker, and he would not grow tired with weary legs.

Dahlin hopped onto Quaesitor's back and held on to his mane. The three little birds were also allowed to sit on his back when they grew tired. Felix, though, indicated to Dahlin that it would fly high into the sky in search of any danger.

Dahlin inspected the map and found a marking not far away that would put the mountain of their destination straight ahead. He told Quaesitor where to go. Quaesitor trotted off onto the path, keeping a steady pace.

They were now going uphill, and the path was steep, but Quaesitor took it with ease. They followed the path for several days, and every night they were fortunate to find shelter and plenty of wild fruits to eat and water to drink. Dahlin had eaten all the food given to him by Karlene.

The weather was turning cold and cloudy, and soon it was snowing gently.

They entered an open space covered in rocks and boulders with little grass. Dahlin carried the birds in his breast pockets to keep them warm. There had been no sign of Felix.

The snow fell fiercely, and soon it was a storm. Dahlin feared for their safety and whispered into Quaesitor's ear. He darted forward and headed for a large outcrop of rocks and discovered a cave into which they all could fit. They sheltered there while the storm raged.

Night descended and it was dark. They could not light a fire, nor did they have any food to eat. Dahlin gave the birds a little water from his flask.

Dahlin took the blanket from his backpack and asked Quaesitor to lie down. They rested on his chest and covered themselves with the blanket. They were safe and warm. Dahlin felt this was a blessing, even though they were surrounded by the harshness of the weather. They all slept peacefully.

Meanwhile, Felix had been flying high in the sky looking for his wayward brothers. He had been searching for some time when he saw two black shapes headed in his direction. It was the ravens.

They reached Felix and dived at him fiercely with their beaks clacking as they tried to bite and peck him. He easily outmanoeuvred them and flew in the opposite direction of Dahlin's position.

They pursued him, but he glided away some distance, then stopped and hovered in the air, waiting for them to reach him.

They saw this as an opportunity to attack an easy target. Just before they reached him, Felix did a somersault and pecked both birds gently on their backs. They turned and hovered before him, surprised that he had not hit them harder.

He spoke to them in raven-speak to leave Rensin and follow a path of peace. They laughed and indicated that they would never leave Rensin and would always serve him.

Felix shook his head in disbelief at their foolishness. They cawed at him, saying that they knew where Dahlin was headed and that his trick to lead them away had failed.

They were about to attack Felix again, but he soared at great speed higher into the sky.

Ravens can reach great altitudes, but the two ravens dared not chase Felix again for they feared he had gone out of their reach. Instead, they flew back to Rensin's fortress to inform him of their findings. This took them a couple of days, as they stopped to rest and find food along the way.

Felix watched them depart and resolved to find Dahlin as quickly as he could to warn him of the coming danger.

The sunlight woke Dahlin in the morning. There was snow lying everywhere, but it was melting quickly, and there were puddles that Quaesitor was able to drink to satisfy his thirst. Dahlin filled his flask, and the birds darted about, warming themselves and finding seeds to eat. Dahlin was hungry, but not so much that it compelled him to eat seeds!

They set off again on the path as it wound its way over the hills and through the trees. Here Dahlin found some wild fruits to eat, and Quaesitor found grasses to fill his belly. He neighed in delight.

Dahlin called a stop after they had travelled for several hours. He jumped from Quaesitor's back and walked over to some rocks that were on top of one another - largest to smallest.

"These have been deliberately placed as a cairn," suggested Dahlin.

The little birds tweeted that they did not understand.

"Sorry," Dahlin answered. "Cairn means a pile of rocks left as a maker. You have learnt a new word," he laughed. The birds twittered in reply.

"Perhaps this is the marker that the map indicated." Dahlin looked at the cairn then saw there was a trail of pebbles that headed into the trees. He turned to his companions.

"This may not make any sense to you, but I know we must follow the pebbles. They will lead us to where I must go."

They did not need Dahlin to give them a reason; they indicated that they would go wherever he took them. Dahlin sensed this, and it gave his heart a feeling of joy.

They followed the pebble trail for the rest of the day. Dahlin had to walk beside Quaesitor as the trees and shrubbery were too close for him to sit on the horse's back. The little birds jumped from bush to bush and branch to branch eating a little from what they could find.

The pebble trail ended as they came out of the forest. They stopped and looked with awe and amazement at the scene before them. They were on a hill above a valley that stretched as far as they could see. It was all beautifully green with pastures, a vineyard, orchards, and gardens. In the middle was a small cottage enclosed by a flowery garden. A little stream flowed beside the cottage, filling into a pond that exited on the other side towards the trees. There were ducks swimming and quacking in the pond.

The sun was shining but near to setting as evening was approaching. The air was warmer. To their right, Dahlin saw a gradual slope leading into the valley. They followed this down and entered onto a pasture. Quaesitor raced off to exercise the weariness out of his limbs and stopped occasionally to partake of the grasses. He neighed in delight. The little birds, Animo, Intrepidus, and Vigilans, flew to the orchard and enjoyed the fruits from its trees. There they met other birds, and Dahlin could hear much happy tweeting and singing.

Dahlin let them go as he sensed no danger. It seemed to him that this valley was hidden from strangers, and only those invited were welcomed. Dahlin wondered how he knew that. It almost felt like home.

He walked towards the cottage and looked to see if there was anyone inside. The flowery garden was an abundance of colour, and he stood and took it in for a few minutes. There were butterflies, bees and other insects tending the garden.

He knocked on the door, but no one answered. The door opened by itself, and Dahlin sensed this as a welcome and an invitation to enter. So, he did, with a smile on his face.

He took his pack from his back and placed it near the table. He could feel a sense of lightness overtake the tiredness in his body. He looked around and discovered a bedroom with a straw mattress and a pillow of feathers. At the back of the cottage was a small stable, which Quaesitor had already discovered. Dahlin patted him as he drank from the trough. The little birds flew to Dahlin and rested on his shoulders. They tweeted to him of all the new friends they had made, then flew off again.

He went back into the cottage and found a pot of flour on the bench next to a wood-burning oven. There was plenty of wood stored near the oven. There was also a pot of olive oil and a collection of cooking and eating implements. Over the sink was a water pump.

Dahlin decided to make some scones. He got the stove warming while he mixed the dough. He made three scones and put them in the oven to cook. They would not take long.

While they were cooking, he explored the cottage. Feeling it was reserved for the cottage's owner, he did not go upstairs. There were only three rooms downstairs. The large eating and cooking area, the bedroom, and a small washroom. To his surprise, there were clean towels and even soap. He decided to give himself a good wash.

When he finished, he could smell that the scones were cooked, so he placed two of them on a plate on the table with a cup of water. He looked through the cupboards and found some honey, which he spread over the scones. He sat at the table and enjoyed this simple meal. He noticed in the corner a bookcase containing several hand-bound books and some scrolls.

He went over to the bookcase and looked through one of the books. It was in a language he did not understand. He thought the letters looked familiar, but he could not recognise the words. He examined some of the other books and scrolls and discovered they were all written in the same language. How very strange, he pondered.

He went outside and looked up into the starry sky. The stars seemed to twinkle like exultant eyes. As he turned to go back inside, he noticed a light coming from somewhere up the mountain. The map had indicated that Hermitage was not far; perhaps the light came from there. He decided to investigate once the sun rose the next day.

He retired to the bedroom and found the bed was very comfortable. He quickly fell into a very peaceful sleep.

Next morning he rose with the rising sun and sang his song of praise. Animo, Intrepidus and Vigilans were also awake, and they sang with him. Dahlin could hear Quaesitor snoring, so he let him be.

He ate the third scone with some honey for his breakfast and a little water. He decided to leave his backpack in the cottage, then walked towards the orchard.

His little birds flew down to him, but he said, "You can stay here with your new friends. I'm going for a walk. Don't be afraid, I am sure I will be safe." They were comforted by his words and flew back to the orchard.

He filled his flask with water and put it into one of his large pockets, and walk towards the mountain. He entered the trees and saw a stairway. This made his climb easier, and he soon came across a passageway which entered the mountain.

Sunlight came through holes in the roof of the passageway as its gradient ascended in a gentle rise. There was only one path which wound its way up, so there was no possibility of getting lost.

He walked for about twenty minutes, as he was being cautious, but he did not need to be, as there were no holes or dips to trap an unwary step. He discovered writing on the walls every ten steps. It was in the same language as the books in the cottage, so he could not understand their message.

The passageway ended at a wooden door. Dahlin stopped and looked intently at the writing engraved all over the door. He knew the letters but not the words. He thought to himself that this was very strange. He was mystified at his inability to read the words.

He reached out his hand to knock, then stopped and lowered his arm.

He looked around; no one was behind him. There was only a gentle breeze of fresh air. He turned back to the door and put his hand on the handle and pushed it down. He let it go, and the door opened wide.

He entered and saw another door on the opposite side. He slowly looked around. The room was decorated brightly with colourful hanging drapes; a fireplace with a fire burning warmly; a table with a light blue tablecloth and a vase of the most wonderful flowers. The flowers looked like those that surrounded the cottage in the valley. There were chairs and a bookcase. Paintings of scenery and people were hung on one of the walls. He sensed he knew the people but did not know their names. The floor was covered with carpets decorated with scenes of nature. It all looked very homely and cosy. The person who lived here would be happy.

Over by a window, he saw a woman dressed in a long white dress with a blue shawl over her head.

"Welcome, Dahlin," said the woman as she turned towards him. She held out her hands in greeting.

Though she was old, her face shone with a smile of youthful loveliness.

Dahlin stood mesmerised.

Seventh

Meanwhile the two ravens had reached Rensin's fortress and flew through the open window and landed on the table as Rensin was eating a morning meal. They started excitedly croaking their report. Rensin held up his hand for them to stop.

"Slow down. You're babbling. You act as if you had experienced a fright or a fight. Which is it?"

They spoke in raven-talk of their encounter with their brother and interrupted each other while not wanting to say they were defeated by him.

"So, he has turned against us. He may suffer for that if I find him," threatened Rensin.

The ravens indicated the direction Dahlin had taken towards the mountain and that the snow would have slowed him down.

"Ah, he has found the place he was searching for. I know where that is. It is a treacherous climb up the cliff face. I will take my horse and ride there rapidly." He reached for his sword.

"And this," waving the sword in the air, "will end his journey." Rensin laughed and the ravens joined in with their cackle.

Rensin was unaware of the secret valley where Dahlin was resting.

Rensin rode on the horse he had stolen and followed the path to the mountain. The ravens flew above, prepared to warn him of any dangers. They travelled all day with few stops. The horse grew weary.

At nightfall Rensin tied the horse to a nearby tree and let it eat the grass within its reach. It drank from a small puddle of water at the base of the tree.

He rested in his tent and left the ravens on watch by the campfire. He knew there were wolves about in the forest and wanted the ravens to warn him if any approached.

During the night, the campfire went out as the ravens had fallen asleep and had not kept it fuelled. Bright eyes looked through the bushes and saw the ravens sleeping and the tent now unprotected.

Three wolves approached silently and slowly. One approached the tent and peered in and saw the sleeping Rensin whose sword was on the ground by his bed. The wolf eyed it for a moment, went forward and took the blade in its teeth and dragged it towards the tent flap. The sword scratched the ground, and Rensin woke suddenly and saw what the wolf was attempting to do. He grabbed the hilt of the sword and swung it at the wolf, but it had already fled the tent.

At the same time, the two other wolves had approached the two sleeping ravens, who, with their acute hearing, heard the footsteps and flew hastily into the tree branches above. They cawed at the wolves, who replied with snarls. The two wolves saw the other wolf fleeing the tent and quickly followed it into the bushes.

Rensin stormed out of his tent waving his sword in the air. Upon seeing the fleeing wolves, swore at them in his anger. The black horse neighed in fear. He looked up at the sheltering ravens in the tree.

"You have failed in your duty to keep the fire burning! I told you there were wolves in this forest."

Then to himself, "It was strange behaviour of that one who tried to steal my sword. Why did it attempt that?"

Rensin did not sleep for the rest of the night, so he decided to leave at first light. The ravens flew above on patrol.

After two hours travel, he came across Sevel's farm and rode his horse up to the house. Sevel saw him and came out of the house in a furious temper.

"What do you want? I don't need any farm helpers. The last one was a pest," he screeched at Rensin.

"I don't want to help you," retorted Rensin. "The last one? What do you mean by the last one?" he sternly asked.

Sevel was taken fearfully aback in meeting someone angrier than he.

"Was he short?" demanded Rensin.

"Why should I answer your questions? I don't want you to meddle in my business," replied Sevel.

Rensin dismounted and stood facing Sevel staring him down. Sevel faulted.

"Yes, he was here a couple of days. I can't remember his name. He was useless, couldn't even fix my fence. And worst of all he stole my horse!" exclaimed Sevel gathering back some of his anger.

Rensin looked resolutely at Sevel and raised his sword and pointed it at the farmer's chest.

"Which way did he go? Tell me or my blade may find a spot you wouldn't like pierced," threatened Rensin.

Sevel faulted again and said pointing north. "That way, a few days ago." He stepped back and his foot touched a log of wood. He continued, "What about my horse? I'll pay you something if you get it back for me," he tentatively asked.

"I don't care about your horse," replied Rensin dismissively. "Your information has been of little use to me."

Rensin turned to go. Sevel quickly picked up the log and threw it at Rensin. A raven cried in warning. In a flash, Rensin turned and struck the log with his sword. The log burst into flames and landed in the haystack, setting it alight.

Sevel gasped and ran back to his house and locked the door.

Rensin laughed and mounted his horse. He found the path again and headed off at a brisk trot. When they saw he had left, Sevel and Karlene rushed from the house and beat the fire out before it consumed the fences.

Rensin soon reached the *Winding Water* and saw that it was a fast-flowing river. He approached the fallen bridge and muttered.

"I see his footprints in the sand. I hope this river has not taken my foe."

He decided to cross the river to check the bank on the other side for any signs of Dahlin. He forcefully made his horse swim at a great pace to prevent them from being dragged downstream by the current. The horse was strong, and in a few minutes, they were across.

Rensin dismounted and examined the sand. He could see Dahlin's footprints and the claw marks of a raven.

"What has that wayward, stupid raven done helping my enemy. He will pay a severe price for his folly." Rensin muttered this threat under his breath.

He also noticed hoof-prints from another horse.

"It would seem Dahlin did steal that idiot farmer's horse after all." And Rensin laughed.

The ravens flew down and in raven-speak informed Rensin they had lost sight of Dahlin. He had disappeared.

"You are foolish birds. He knows how to hide even from your sight. I sense he is not far. He has gone to the mountain, and that is where we shall go at great speed."

He forced his horse into a gallop, and they raced along the path. Soon they reached the cairn, but before Rensin could see it, all the stones fell to the ground, hiding the direction Dahlin had taken.

It started to snow.

After several hours, Rensin halted, and his exhausted horse breathed out a cloud of white air. He had reached the bottom of the mountain and looked up at its steep peak and could just see the shape of a castle jutting out from the sheer rocky side. The snow swirled around him as it grew in strength.

"Nobody could climb up to that castle. It is too vertical. There are no hand holds." He muttered to himself angrily, then he realised, "There must be another way. I must find it." He looked around but could see nothing as the snow had covered the ground and was getting worse.

Unexpectedly, a stone hit him on his head. Rensin moved back. Several more stones fell on him.

He glanced up and saw that a side of the mountain had broken away, and the rocks were falling directly upon him.

He grabbed the reins of his horse and forcefully dug his boots into its side to make it move out of the way as quickly as possible. The horse was exhausted, but it too did not want to be crushed under a stony rubble. It sprinted back to the path and the protection of the trees. It galloped for some time, barely able to see through the snowy storm. Rensin angrily urged it on, whipping it forcefully.

The snowstorm weakened, but the snow still fell, making it uncomfortable for Rensin. He was wet and shivering. He decided to stop at Sevel's farm for food, warmth, and dry clothes.

It took longer to reach Sevel's farmhouse as the horse could only proceed at a walking pace. It had struggled getting across the Winding Water, and they were taken downstream for some distance but managed, after great effort, to reach the other side.

Rensin did not let the horse rest and continued to the farmhouse during the night. It was dark, and the horse became fearful.

Rensin was concerned that the wolves might make another attack, and in his weakened condition would not be able to fend them off.

Meanwhile back at the farm, Sevel and Karlene were exhausted and covered in black soot after putting out the fire.

Sevel fell to his knees and wept.

"What have I done?" he cried. "I feel so ashamed. I was cruel to Dahlin. I couldn't say to him that his work on the fence was well done, in fact better than I could have done. And now I have told that beast of a man where to find him." Sevel collapsed onto the ground.

Karlene stood amazed at the unexpected outburst from her husband. Never had she seen him remorseful about any of his bad habits. She tentatively walked over to him and placed her hand on his back. He sobbed louder. She bent down and held him in her arms. He turned and looked into her eyes.

"I am sorry for the cruelness of my behaviour to

you, my love. Yes, you are my love. You should have left me long ago. I don't deserve you. Will you forgive me?" he implored.

She thought quietly for a moment, then took a deep breath.

"I could accuse you of much, but I won't. Ever since I met Dahlin my mind and heart have changed. Somehow his presence took away the curtness and roughness within me," she quietly replied.

She helped Sevel to stand and embraced him and whispered into his ears.

"I forgive you completely. I never want to talk about any of our bad behaviour again," she cried into his chest.

They kept hugging and sobbing together for several minutes, then Sevel spoke urgently.

"We must leave here now. I fear Rensin will return, and he will punish us for his failure to find Dahlin." Sevel held Karlene's hand as they walked quickly back to the house.

"How do you know?" asked Karlene.

"I saw snow on the mountain and that will make Rensin turn back. That mountain does strange things. Gather as much of our supplies as you can while I harness the horses to the wagon," he urged.

Karlene and Sevel hurried to get their escape plan into action. Within a short time, they were on the wagon and headed towards Sunatin.

"We can stay at my sister's farm. Since her husband died, she is struggling to manage the farm and what with her four children, she will need our help," suggested Karlene.

"That's a good idea. I've been neglectful of your sister," replied Sevel.

"I have left something for Rensin that'll surprise him," she said, "I left wood by the fire and some food on the table." She chuckled.

Sevel laughed heartedly for the first time in years.

"I never thought we would pay back meanness with kindness," he said and laughed again.

"Also, Dahlin did not steal the stallion. I saw it jump the fence and escape from the yard and run across the field. I guess it will find more kindness in Dahlin than it ever did from me," admitted Sevel.

Karlene patted Sevel on his knee.

"There are many things we must make amends for to others. We will do it together and cheerfully," she suggested.

Sevel nodded his head in agreement.

Some time later, Rensin found his way to Sevel's farm. It was dark and cloudy, but his eyes were sharp. At the front door, he dismounted from his horse; it collapsed exhausted to the ground. He stopped and listened, but he could hear no sound except the wind through the trees. He decided to be cautious, prepared for a trap. He kicked open the door, its rattling shaking the silence in the house.

He looked around the room. There was a pile of wood near the fireplace, which was already prepared to be set alight. He took his sword and smashed the wood in the fireplace, and it burst into flames.

On the table there was placed a loaf of bread, some fruit, dried meat, and a jug of wine. He picked up the bread and sniffed it, broke a piece off, and threw it to his ravens. They greedily ate it and asked for more. Rensin waited a minute to see if the ravens grew ill. They kept cawing for more. Confident that the food was safe, Rensin ate as greedily as the ravens. He drank all the wine, then fell asleep on the rug before the fire, which warmed away the bitterness of his defeat at the mountain.

He did not notice the black eyes that watched him from a tree outside the window.

Eighth

Dahlin stood in silence while he looked at the wonderful woman before him. He waited for her to speak again.

She smiled. He smiled.

"My name is Marin, come over to me," she said simply.

Dahlin walked slowly but gently towards her. He felt his heart beating faster. His mind was thinking that this was somehow familiar, something he had done in the past. But how could that be?

"If you had knocked, I would not have let you in, but I knew *you* wouldn't," she emphasised the 'you' as if she knew all about him. Dahlin's mind was feeling wonderful rather than anxious.

"How do you know about me? Why do I feel like I should know you? What is this place? Do you live alone?" the questions bubbled out of Dahlin.

Marin held up her hand.

"Do not be afraid," she said peacefully.

"Now kneel before me for only one time, as it is necessary," she asked gently.

Dahlin felt neither hesitancy nor fear. He was overcome by a presence of peace. A peace that he had never felt before.

He knelt before Marin. She raised her hands

high above her head, looking up as if she could see something or someone looking down. She placed her hands on Dahlin's head. He felt the softness of her hands, and it reminded him of a mother's touch. His mother.

Marin looked at Dahlin and closed her eyes, she seemed to go into a trance. She spoke in a prayerful voice, words that were melodious and, in some way, familiar to Dahlin. He felt he had to let go and completely trust. He closed his eyes.

Dahlin was not aware of time passing, he later discovered it was over two hours.

He felt a gentle breeze about him and sensed a bright light surrounding them. He was perfectly still. A soft warmth went through him. He heard Marin's voice and slowly the words became clear. He could understand. It was a familiar language. A language he knew.

She sang a prayer of healing, thanksgiving and praise.

He fell asleep, and Marin carefully put him onto the rug and covered him with a white blanket. She went over to a bench and started preparing a meal of fruits, bread, and some cooked fish.

Dahlin slept for a short time. He opened his eyes and saw Marin sitting at the table looking at him with her gentle eyes. He felt a comfort he had not experienced for a long time. It was like being home.

He got up off the floor and folded the white

blanket and placed it on a chair, and walked over to the table.

"You had many questions, Dahlin. Do you have more?" she asked.

"They don't seem to matter anymore. I feel that I know you," responded Dahlin.

He paused and reflected and realised that his mind was now clear. Marin's healing prayer and the light that had surrounded them had cast away the haze his mind had suffered for the past year. Though there were some things he did not know. He looked steadily at Marin, then his eyes brightened in realisation.

"You are my Grandmother!" he exclaimed.

He ran into her arms and held her in a hug of softness. She returned his hug and kissed him on his forehead. After a little while, he let her go and sat beside her at the table. He saw all the food on the table and realised that he was hungry. Marin anticipated his request.

"Yes, you can eat. And while we share this meal, I will answer some of your questions. Then I suggest you go to bed, and you will have a good night's rest, and we will talk more in the morning." She waited while he ate some food.

"You asked if I live alone. Yes, I do mostly. But in the cottage more than in this castle. I only come here when I need to. I have a friend, a trader, who brings me supplies. I give him some of my produce from the orchard and vineyard, and in return, he gives me cloth for my sewing and grains for my baking. He lives in a town further north and knows the way through the forest." She stopped speaking and held Dahlin's gaze.

"Thank you for the food and the answer to one of my questions. I am feeling very tired, and my mind is trying to recover its memories. I can sense them, but I feel there are gaps. Tomorrow I will know more. You, my dearest Grandmother, will help me learn more about myself and my new purpose," said Dahlin.

He rose from his chair and kissed Marin on the cheek, curled up in the blanket in front of the fire, and was soon asleep.

Marin cleared the table, then sat in a chair by the fire. She looked down at Dahlin and sighed.

"You have much more to do, and the strength building up inside of you will come alive, and you will bring peace to many. You will endure the hardships that are to come with the brightness that shines within you," she said to herself as she drifted off to sleep.

Dahlin woke as the rays of the sun came through the window. The fire was burning low, so he fed it with the logs from the crate. It soon grew new flames and warmed the room.

He saw that Marin was still sleeping and quietly opened the door to the balcony and closed it again as he went out. It was a clear day dawning, and he could see far. He thought he could make out the smoke from fires burning in Sunatin. That brought back memories of the carpenter and the cobbler who had befriended him and provided for his needs. He knew he would see them again.

He went back inside to see Marin getting ready to leave.

"We will go back to the cottage for breakfast, as there are more food supplies there. We will talk on the way," she said as she gave him a morning smile.

He welcomed this, as he wished to see his friends again to assure them that he was safe.

"I would welcome the walk with some talk," he laughed.

Marin laughed too, and they set off through the passageway. They held hands but did not say anything until they entered the sunlight. They paused and took in the scene before them and said their morning thanks and praise.

"I will tell you of what happened a year ago. It is tragic. You and I are of the Pentahaven Peoples. We live in this area of the valley and further north. We are a peaceful people. We grow food for our needs and share it with those who come to us. Your mother used to live here with me, but when she married, she moved north one day's journey by wagon. She was very happy, and her husband is a wonderful man. Soon they had two children, you and your sister, Janne. Your parents are Joimer and Maemey. Do you remember their names?" asked Marin.

"Only now that you have spoken does my mind see them, and I feel the love that is in our family," Dahlin replied softly. "Something happened to us, but my memory is misty. Please go on," he requested.

"Misty is an accurate word to describe it," continued Marin. "The Gallen people, who live in the south, were exploring our area and were received with kindness. But they had a deep distrust of others that our presence could not influence. They produced a poisonous mist that left many of us unconscious, including your family. They took about two hundred of our people. Fortunately, many had escaped into the hills. Our people were taken in the Gallen's wagons down to their lands to toil in their fields like slaves." Marin paused because Dahlin had stopped walking. He was staring at her.

"I remember. It was cruelty that we had never known. As we were being carried away, I awoke when we were going around Sunatin. My father wrapped me in his blanket, then spoke softly to me and warned me to be ready when we turned the next bend. As the wagon turned, he looked to see if we were unobserved. The guard had looked in another direction, and my father said, 'Save us.' I could hear my mother and sister crying as he quickly threw me out of the wagon into the bushes. The blanket helped to soften my landing, and I rolled into a bush but hit my head on a rock and fell into unconsciousness. The guards didn't see me as I was covered in the foliage. When I woke up, several hours had passed, and I could remember little. I didn't know where I was. But two things stayed in my memory. Go north and find Hermitage," said Dahlin sadly.

"You have remembered well, Dahlin," said Marin. "I will tell you more about 'our presence' and its influence on others but do you remember it?" she asked.

"Yes, I do. Since you healed me, memories have been awakening in my mind. It is that some of us, not all, are born with an intuitive ability. We seem to know. Also, our presence creates harmony in others who are open to it. Not all are influenced by it. In fact, some become quite hostile, like Rensin and the Gallen peoples. I wonder if it is true for all of them?" pondered Dahlin in reply.

"You will find out. But I will not speak of that now. You have a task that will come shortly. Let's keep walking to the cottage and I will prepare you breakfast. Look, I can see your friends fast approaching. Greet them and we will talk later," suggested Marin.

Dahlin looked across the pastures and saw Animo, Intrepidus and Vigilans flying swiftly towards him. Not far behind was Quaesitor galloping at great speed. When they reached him, the birds sang in delight and Quaesitor nudged him playfully. This lifted Dahlin's spirits as he was feeling the sadness of his family's plight.

They reached the cottage and, while Marin was preparing breakfast, Dahlin went over to the corner bookcase and browsed through the books. He discovered he could now read the language. It was his language. They were handwritten by his ancestors and by Marin. He felt that he would write a book too later in life, and it would be placed in the bookcase for others to read.

During the morning, they talked for a while in the cottage and after a light lunch went for a walk in the orchard and vineyard.

"Who cares for the land and all its produce?" asked Dahlin, who was amazed at the quality and abundance of the fruits.

"I care for it as best I can manage at my age, but I do hire some labourers from the northern village of *Heathertown*. They all know the way here but keep the path secret from strangers. Nature does its part too; all the insects and scurrying creatures love to bustle about too," laughed Marin.

"I am finding it hard to laugh now that I have remembered the suffering of my family," mourned Dahlin.

"You must still be able to laugh even when your heart is sorrowful, or your hope and joy will disappear. Have hope, Dahlin, and trust that what is within you will bear fruit. Your courage will grow, and then nothing will defeat you," heartened Marin.

Marin's words lifted Dahlin's spirits, and he felt a deep sense of peace and encouragement in her presence.

"I wanted to ask you about the gifts of our

people. Why are we able to cause a change in mood and emotion in others, either for good or bad, as in Rensin?" asked Dahlin.

"When did you become aware of your ability?" inquired Marin.

"When I awoke, after being thrown from the wagon, I didn't know where I was or even who I was. I wandered around for some time, hiding from others and eating off the land and sleeping in caves or branch huts that I built. I couldn't avoid people all the time, and when they surprised me by their presence, I was afraid. But they didn't hurt me; they helped me. At first, I just thought people were kind, but then I came across others who were suddenly hostile to me, and I ran away from them. Some of them chased me and cried out that they were sorry they'd hurt me. They gave me food and shelter. I realised that it was something in me that was affecting them," explained Dahlin.

"And when you discovered that, what did you do?" questioned Marin.

"At first, I was afraid that I would misuse the ability just to get what I could out of people. But I knew that would be a selfish and malicious thing to do. I couldn't do that; it felt it was against my nature," admitted Dahlin, and he looked at the ground.

"Look up Dahlin, you discovered your nature even when you didn't know who you were," and she laughed again.

Dahlin laughed too. He felt a great sense of

tranquillity. He stood close to Marin and hugged her gently and shed a few tears.

Later that day, they walked from the cottage, through the passageway and back into the castle.

"Why did you want to return here?" asked Dahlin.

"You need to see something," replied Marin.

They entered the room where Dahlin had been healed, and he felt a deep comfort in recalling that experience. Marin walked over to the door across the room and picked up the white blanket from the chair on which Dahlin had folded it.

"Here you will need this," she said as she gave him the blanket. Dahlin wrapped it around his shoulders.

She opened the door; a cold breeze blew in with some scattering snow.

"Go outside onto the balcony that overhangs the steep side of the mountain. It is quite safe. Look down and you will see a horse and a rider looking up," directed Marin.

Dahlin did as she asked, as he completely trusted her but was puzzled by her request. He tightly wrapped the blanket around him and went outside. The snow was falling stronger. He looked down over the balcony and saw a horse and a rider, as Marin had said he would. Though he was far up the mountain, he could see that it was Rensin. Then the snow grew fiercer, and stones and rocks began to fall towards

Rensin, who ducked and weaved out of the way. Dahlin gasped and called to Marin, who was standing just inside the door.

"I don't want Rensin harmed by the falling rubble!" exclaimed Dahlin.

"Do not worry, Dahlin, he will not be hurt by any of the rocks. He will escape thinking it was his skill that nothing injured him. If the mountain had wanted to, he would have been struck by the first falling stones. I knew you would not want Rensin injured, so he has not been," replied Marin.

Dahlin watched until Rensin had urged his horse to gallop away. He re-entered the room, closed the door, folded the blanket, and placed it on the chair.

Marin had the fire burning.

"Come and warm yourself and tell me your thoughts," said Marin.

Dahlin sat on the floor in front of the fire and warmed his hands while he made sense of his feelings.

"Now that you have returned my memories and told me of my life before our people's entrapment, I know what I must do." Dahlin paused. "Rensin is a troubled man, and his bitterness feeds his anger against me. And against everyone too!"

Dahlin looked up at Marin questioningly. She smiled at him.

"You have already said, 'I know what to do', but I assume you mean specifics. I can't tell you those as I don't know them myself. All I know for sure is that at the time you must act, you will be given the light to know how to act." She laughed at her puzzling reply.

Dahlin realised this too and laughed with her.

The afternoon was getting late, so they decided to walk back to the cottage before the darkness of night fell. As they entered the pastures of the valley, Dahlin's friends rushed towards them. The birds tweeted and sang joyfully to see them. Quaesitor fell on all his knees and offered his back to Marin if she wished a ride home to the cottage.

She laughed and accepted his offer, and sat side-saddle and held his mane for support, but Quaesitor knew the dignity of Marin and rose and walked carefully without ruffling her dress. Dahlin walked beside them as the birds flew around in circles over their heads, singing a joyful song.

Dahlin stayed with Marin in the cottage for two weeks, and in that time, he read some of her books, enjoyed long walks with his friends, and talked often with Marin by the fire.

One day during the first week, Dahlin saw a black shape flying high in the sky, and it was descending towards him. He knew it was Felix because, by befriending the raven, it would sense where he was and find him anywhere, including this hidden valley. He waited with his arm outstretched, and Felix landed on it within a short time.

"Hello, Felix, I am happy to see you again. Do you have news to tell me?" asked Dahlin.

Felix spoke in raven-speak which, since his healing, Dahlin now fully understood. Felix spoke and this is his story.

Felix was not far from Rensin when he was at the base of the mountain and galloped away on his horse. Rensin was pushing the horse hard to get back to Sevel's farm before nightfall. When they arrived, it was exhausted, but Rensin left it in the yard enclosure without providing it with any food. It found a few scraps and there was some water in the trough. Felix rested nearby, perched in a tree over the farmhouse.

The next morning, Rensin rode again on the horse towards his fortress. He pushed the horse too hard, and suddenly it reared up and threw him to the ground. It gave him a hard kick on his leg and raced off in the opposite direction.

Rensin lay stunned on the ground for some time. He slowly got to his feet and tottered limply on the path to his fortress. He was hoping to pass a traveller and force a ride, but no one came his way. It took him three days of laboured walking, and he arrived at his fortress dishevelled and hungry. His temper was fierce. Felix could hear him yelling at his brother ravens, and they suddenly flew out of a window towards the mountain in search of Dahlin again.

Felix concluded by assuring Dahlin that they would not find him hidden here in this valley.

Dahlin thanked Felix for the news and the effort he exerted in discovering it. He held Felix in his arms and took him to the cottage to give him some food and water, also to meet Marin.

"Who is this wonderful bird," exclaimed Marin as they entered the cottage.

"This is Felix, he has told me of the poor condition of Rensin after his fleeing from the mountain. We are safe here as he doesn't know the whereabouts of this valley," replied Dahlin.

"Nor shall he," confirmed Marin.

She was thrilled to meet the raven and took him in her arms and talked softly to him for several minutes. She then let Felix go, and he flew out of the window towards the orchard where he was greeted by the three little birds and their new friends. It was a strange sight!

Dahlin looked out of the window and saw Quaesitor approaching the orchard to greet Felix.

"You have some wonderful friends, Dahlin. It is a quality of your gift that animals sense. Some more easily than others. Ravens are one of the hardest, and yet you have calmed one, and it is now dedicated to you. Do you know if there are any other animals befriending you?" asked Marin as she joined him at the window.

"I have a feeling there is another, but I haven't met it yet," replied Dahlin, remembering the morning campfire that started by itself.

The following week was calm and peaceful.

Dahlin thought to himself that the green valley, with the presence of his companions and his loving Grandmother, was the most wonderful place he had been. But he knew he had to leave it soon to face his foe.

When he returned, he would devise a plan with Marin to rescue his family and all those enslaved by the Gallens.

Ninth

A few days later, Dahlin rose with the sun and sang his song kneeling in the garden outside the cottage. He listened to the silence being transformed by the singing birds and insects. He felt peaceful, and his health had improved. His mind was clear, and his purpose was strong. This was the day he had to leave and confront Rensin.

He sensed Marin approaching and rose to his feet. She stood by his side and took his hand in hers.

"I will not tell you how to act for I am aware that you already know. Our people always know that gentleness is greater than anger and hatred. Forgiveness heals revenge and even death," she spoke these words from the depth of her heart.

"Thank you, my dearest Grandmother Marin. The treasure of your presence will be gold in my heart. I will have some breakfast then leave with Quaesitor. Riding with him will shorten the journey," said Dahlin looking into her eyes.

"Breakfast is ready, and I have filled your backpack with supplies. Will the birds go with you too?" she asked.

"I haven't asked them, but I feel they will come. I don't think I could stop them," and they both laughed.

When it was time to go, Dahlin and Marin

hugged for a short time. Dahlin jumped on Quaesitor's back and the birds flew into the air above them. Dahlin turned and waved to Marin, and she waved in return.

Quaesitor cantered towards the hidden path and soon they were out of sight.

Marin decided to go to the mountain castle in a couple of days to view the events from the balcony. Her longsightedness enabled her to see far. The weather had cleared and there would be no more snow.

Dahlin and his companions made good progress and were soon at Sevel's farm. They saw the burnt area surrounding the haystack and felt concerned for Sevel and Karlene. Dahlin dismounted Quaesitor and cautiously entered the house. The house was in disarray with plates, cups and other implements thrown about. The fireplace was full of ash with much of it scattered over the floor.

"I don't think Karlene would have left her house in such a state as this. Someone else has done this and I know it was Rensin," Dahlin said to his bird friends who had flown into the house when he entered.

Quaesitor went and looked at his stable, but it was undamaged. He saw that the wagon and the other horses had left.

Dahlin spent the rest of the day tidying and cleaning, and his birds helped as much as they could.

By sunset, the house was in a better condition. Dahlin ate some of the food Marin had given him, and the birds and Quaesitor found food outside in the pasture. Dahlin lit a fire and warmed the house. They all stayed the night.

In the morning, they set off towards Rensin's fortress. Dahlin decided not to hide their presence, and he soon saw Rensin's ravens above. Having seen him the ravens raced back to report to their master.

"Do not go after them Felix," Dahlin stopped his raven from flying after his brothers. "Soon you will have an encounter with them. Prepare for it calmly and you may win them back," advised Dahlin.

The two ravens flew through the open fortress window and almost knocked Rensin over with their urgent message that they had found Dahlin. They were nearly breathless but reported that Dahlin was walking on the path not far from the *Winding Water* and was headed directly for the fortress.

"What is that fool doing? Has he come to confront me?" Rensin sneered. "Come, my servants, let us not disappoint him and finish our day with success!"

Rensin took up his sword and whetted its blade to deadly sharpness. He strode out of the fortress dressed in his blackest leather and boots, with the ravens in fast pursuit.

Felix had been searching the skies, since seeing his brothers, on alert for any danger ahead. He soon saw them flying above Rensin. He flew down to Dahlin and warned him of Rensin's approach.

"Then we shall stop here," said Dahlin to his companions. "We are not far from the stream and its sandy bank. Quaesitor, I want you to hide in the bushes. Don't come out unless I call. Animo, Intrepidus and Vigilans stay perched in the trees above. I don't want you hurt."

Dahlin reached for Felix to perch on his arm. Then spoke to him in a whisper.

"This will be a dangerous time for you. Your brothers will attack you. You must outwit them without harming them. This will confuse their actions, and it will give you time to show that you mean them no harm."

Felix nodded and flew to the nearest tree to await their arrival.

Dahlin stood in the middle of the path and closed his eyes. After a little time, he could hear the approaching sounds and soon heard Rensin's voice.

"You are a fool, Dahlin," shouted Rensin. "I will cut you down with ease. Why do you not have a sword? Do you think I will listen to your pleas? I will not. I no longer want you in this world!"

Rensin rushed at Dahlin with his sword raised and swinging it from side to side, tried to strike. Dahlin easily side-stepped the attack and ran into the bushes and raced for the stream. Rensin was in pursuit cutting away the bushes and branches with his sharp blade.

On the bank of the stream, Dahlin picked up an arm's length piece of driftwood.

Rensin laughed when he saw this feeble attempt to defend against his mighty sword.

Dahlin stood still and held the dry wood raised like a shield. He waited for Rensin's approach.

Rensin paused as he reached the bank of the stream and gave Dahlin a deadly stare.

"You think that brittle piece of wood will hold out for one blow against my fierce blade?" he laughed.

Dahlin did not reply but stood his ground.

Rensin ran at full speed, his sword's blade directed at Dahlin's heart.

Dahlin held up the driftwood, and it glowed white with light. Rensin's sword smashed against it, but to his surprise, his sword slid away to his right. Rensin raised his sword again and struck downwards upon Dahlin, who quickly raised the piece of wood to take the blow. Rensin's sword slid away to his left.

Rensin withdrew for a moment in fury and could not understand why his sword had not shattered the driftwood into a thousand pieces.

Dahlin took this reprieve and ran to the stream stepping ankle-deep into the water. Rensin looked at Dahlin with a snarling grimace and walked determinedly towards him.

This time he aimed at Dahlin with more control. Dahlin held up the driftwood. Rensin's sword struck and pounded at the driftwood, but Dahlin held it firmly in front of his body.

Rensin hammered his sword at Dahlin repeatedly, but it was constantly brushed aside by the driftwood. Each time he struck, it glowed white with light but did not splinter. Rensin was tiring.

"Stop, Rensin, stop! Can't you see that you cannot harm me," called Dahlin, pleading with Rensin to see reason.

"I shall not," screamed Rensin, who furiously ran at Dahlin with his sword raised above his head.

Dahlin quickly moved into deeper water up to his knees. As Rensin entered the water his foot caught in a hole, and he fell to his side onto his sword. Its blade pierced his chest just below his heart.

Rensin screamed but this time in great pain. He staggered out of the water and fell onto the sandy bank. The sword came out of his chest and fell onto the sand.

Rensin did not move but breathed shallowly. Dahlin came out of the water, dropping the driftwood that had protected him. It shattered into a thousand pieces upon the sand. He walked to Rensin's side and looked sadly down upon him.

"Why do you hate me so?" asked Dahlin.

Rensin looked up weakly into Dahlin's sad and pitying eyes.

"Why don't you pick up my sword and kill me? That is the only way you will be rid of my hatred," croaked Rensin.

Dahlin walked around Rensin's body and picked up the sword. He took it in his hands and walked back to Rensin, who looked up into its blade, waiting for it to strike. Instead, Dahlin raised the sword above his head and swung it around, throwing it into the water. For a moment, it floated on the surface, then disintegrated into dust, and its thousands of pieces floated away.

Rensin was bewildered and his thoughts swirled in confusion.

Dahlin sat down beside Rensin and nursed the injured body onto his knees. He touched the wound, and the blood stopped, but the deep gash remained. He took the blanket from his backpack, ripped off a piece, and tied it around Rensin's chest.

Dahlin laid Rensin on the sand to let him rest and sat beside him. Nothing was said for some time. Rensin roused himself weakly.

"Why didn't you kill me?" he asked.

"I do not kill. Each human life is a gift and is precious. Even yours, Rensin!" Dahlin smiled at him. He paused for a minute.

"I forgive you Rensin," said Dahlin simply.

Rensin was overwhelmed. Suddenly he felt sorry. Tears swelled in his eyes falling down his face. He tasted their bitter salt. He felt his animosity and hatred dissolve in his tears. He felt a warmth flood through his body. He raised his hand towards Dahlin who took it and kissed it.

The three little birds flew down and rested on Dahlin's shoulders and sang a gentle tune. Rensin wept openly and fell into a faint.

Meanwhile, in the sky above, Felix was flying out of reach of his brothers. They darted and whizzed around, trying to peck him, but he easily escaped their attacks. He looked down and flew over the stream and saw Rensin lying injured on the sand.

He told his brothers that their master was

defeated but was still alive. Dahlin had spared him. The brother ravens were confused. They did not know what to do. Quickly, Felix flew down towards Rensin. The ravens soared in pursuit to protect their master.

Felix landed by Dahlin, who took him up in his arms.

The brother ravens dropped near Rensin, who awoke and looked at them. "You must become brothers again," he said weakly but decisively.

Instead, the ravens cawed and croaked loudly and flew away. Rensin looked sadly into the sky at their departure.

"Don't be concerned, Rensin, I have been told that a raven's heart takes longer to change. If Felix can change, they too, in time, will change. Have hope that it will happen soon," comforted Dahlin.

"Quaesitor come forward," called Dahlin.

The horse came out of the bushes and sauntered up to Dahlin.

"My horse will carry you on its back when we leave tomorrow, as you are too injured to walk," said Dahlin to Rensin.

They all stayed there for a while as darkness fell, but the moon had risen and gave a peaceful light to the surroundings.

Dahlin wanted to give Rensin a fish to eat to build up his strength when unexpectedly three wolves came out of the bushes. Two were carrying some dead wood that they dropped not far away; another went to the water and soon caught a couple of fish. They made a campfire from stones and started the fire with their claws. They sat on the sand a little distance from Dahlin, who looked at them kindly.

Soon the fish were cooked. Dahlin took a small knife from his backpack and cut some of it off and fed it to Rensin. He also gave him some water to drink.

"You give me more kindness than I deserve," Rensin struggled to say in his weakness. "And you have some amazing friends," he chuckled slowly.

"Yes, I do, and they all choose me," said Dahlin. "Now I will make up a bed with my blankets so that you can have a little comfort as you sleep."

Rensin was soon asleep, so Dahlin joined his friends by the fire and ate some of the fish and some of Marin's food. He felt many things in his heart. Peaceful, now that Rensin was reconciled, and hopeful for the future task of his family's rescue.

The next morning, Dahlin and Rensin set out for Sunatin. Rensin was determined to reconcile with his father, Johan. The journey took them several days as they could not go fast due to Rensin's injuries. Quaesitor carried Rensin, and the three little birds followed, flying from tree to tree. The wolves followed but concealed themselves in the bushes. Felix had left them in search of his brothers, as he hoped to change their hearts.

As they walked along, Dahlin asked Rensin, "I would like to know why you hated me so intensely if it is not too hard for you to recall that memory."

Rensin looked sadly at him and sighed.

"I will tell you what happened, now in shame but also in happiness," replied Rensin, hesitantly. "Several months ago, I was walking in the southern area below Sunatin. It was a wide road, and there were many people and wagons. I was disgruntled and angry at everyone. I had left my father in my bitterness. I remember walking near someone who I now know was you. I felt a sudden burst of anger and hatred. It was like the air I was breathing had been infused with goodness and purity. I sensed it immediately. I hated it. It consumed my feelings and turned me black with rage. It was overwhelming.

"I turned around to find you so that I could attack you, but a wagon came between us, and when it had gone, you were gone. I searched around and bumped into many people who got angry with me, so I had to run off to escape them. For several days I tried to shake off the feelings, but they wouldn't go away. They intensified my miserable condition.

"I fled back to my fortress and gathered my ravens and instructed them to search for you. I also went to my father's workshop, for I sensed that you had been there. The rest you know," concluded Rensin, who hung his head and cried.

Dahlin stopped Quaesitor and hugged Rensin.

"I am sorry to have caused you such pain," said Dahlin.

"You, sorry, no it is I who am sorry. You have forgiven me, and I feel new. My tears are now tears of joy. A joy I have never felt before in my life. And to my surprise, my injuries are healing quickly. Let us hasten to my father, for my heart aches to receive his forgiveness, if he is willing to give it," replied Rensin.

"I know for sure that he will, Rensin, I felt his pain and it was a pain seeking healing and reconciliation," replied Dahlin in encouragement.

That evening they camped by the *Winding Waters*. The wolves hurried about and prepared the meal again, cooking fish on the campfire.

"I've never known wolves to be such great cooks," laughed Rensin.

The wolves looked at Rensin and laughed too. They all laughed, and there was warmth in every heart, not only from the fire.

The sun was shining when they entered Sunatin. Rensin and Dahlin were walking together beside Quaesitor. People in the street recognised Rensin and talked quietly amongst themselves. They were puzzled by Rensin's return, but they feared to ask him.

Dahlin entered Johan's shop and called to him.

"Johan, I have returned to bring you news of great joy," shouted Dahlin.

Johan came out of his workshop and smiled as soon as he saw Dahlin.

"You bring me news of joy! Just seeing you again is joy enough what more could you give me," asked Johan.

Dahlin stepped aside and Rensin entered.

"Ah, my son what has happened to you? Are you injured?" Johan did not know what he was saying as he was confused at the appearance of Rensin.

Rensin fell to his knees with tears flowing down his cheeks and clasped his father's feet. Johan put his hand on Rensin's head and waited for his son to speak.

"Father, forgive me for all the wrong I have done. I no longer deserve to be called your son," started Rensin, but his father interrupted.

"You are my son and will always be my son. Cast from your mind and heart all your bitter past, for you are born again. From today you are my new son, and each day following we will build our family again." He paused. "And I could use some help in the shop," he laughed, tears flowing down his face.

Johan lifted his son from the floor, and they hugged. They cried and laughed at the same time.

"We will have a party and invite the whole town, and you Dahlin will be our guest of honour for bringing my son back to me," and Johan turned to see that Dahlin had gone.

He and Rensin rushed to the door and into the street, calling out Dahlin's name. But they could not find him.

Quaesitor, the birds, and the wolves had all departed too.

Tenth

Dahlin, leading Quaesitor, had quickly walked through the town. As soon as he was on the outskirts and on the pathway, he jumped onto Quaesitor's back and they galloped away as fast as an eagle in flight. Animo, Intrepidus and Vigilans, his faithful little birds, swiftly followed. The wolves had been hiding in the bushes, but when they saw Dahlin leave, they too, speedily followed.

Dahlin wished to get back to Marin as quickly as possible.

They stopped for the evening and set up camp by the *Winding Water*. Dahlin had wild fruits and fish for his meal, while his friends foraged for their own food. He gathered them around the campfire just as the moon was rising.

"My dear friends, we will arrive at the valley in a few days, and I will spend time with Marin planning the rescue of my family and my people. Also, I have other matters I need to learn from her.

"I am now giving you the opportunity to go your own way if you wish. No one needs to follow me on my dangerous mission," Dahlin paused and looked at their faces.

Quaesitor immediately indicated that he would stay with Dahlin.

"Thank you, Quaesitor. I was hoping you would

as I will need your speed and strength."

The birds twittered together for a little time then flew onto Dahlin's shoulders indicating they were going to stay with him.

"Thank you, my dear singing friends. While I am with Marin, you can spend your time in the orchard with your fellow birds and eat to your heart's content."

They chirped an agreeing laugh together.

The wolves took longer to discuss their concerns but decided that one of them would stay with Dahlin, and the others would return to their pack. The wolf who would stay was the first one who helped Dahlin.

"I am most gracious that you have aided me this far and I wish the two of you a safe journey back to your pack."

Dahlin shook each of their paws, and the wolves licked each other's faces, expressing their affection. Then, they ran off into the bushes. Dahlin patted the one wolf that remained.

"I'd like to ask you if you accept the name, Nobilis? For you have shown that you are noble with dignity, worthiness, and honour," asked Dahlin as he held the wolf's paw.

The wolf wagged its tail, then licked Dahlin on the cheek, which indicated his willing acceptance of the name of Nobilis.

They trekked in the same manner for a few days more without incident. It was as if nature itself needed time to be at peace.

Soon they came to the cairn which had rebuilt itself after Rensin's departure. They walked along its hidden path towards the valley.

"I wonder if the valley has a name," thought Dahlin, "I will ask Marin."

Dahlin reflected on everything that had happened to him since his awakening a year ago. He remembered more after being healed by Marin, but he knew he was still young and did not know enough about his people and their strengths and weaknesses.

Marin, being his grandmother, should be able to help him. He did not want to blindly go into a battle with the Gallen people. He needed to know his adversary if he was going to rescue his people. He desired to make peace with the Gallen people as he had with Rensin. However, if they were unreceptive to the influence of his presence and were resistant, what would he do then?

Dahlin silently pondered these matters, and it seemed in little time that they were at the entrance to the valley. He looked down into the vale and breathed its refreshing air. It cleared his fuzzy head, and he felt energised. His companions felt it too and took their leave of Dahlin and raced away to find their new friends and to eat some fresh food.

Dahlin saw Marin waiting at the door of the cottage. She waved to him, and he returned her wave with a happy smile. Nobilis walked by his side.

"Who is this coming now?" asked Marin as Nobilis came walking towards her.

"May I introduce another faithful friend, a wolf I have named Nobilis," replied Dahlin.

Nobilis then trotted happily towards Marin, who knelt and gave the wolf a hug around its neck and patted its back.

"You are indeed a wonderful wolf," she said as she looked into its eyes. Nobilis pressed closer to her and gave a wolfy smile. Marin laughed. She let Nobilis run away to find Quaesitor.

Dahlin and Marin entered the cottage. Dahlin dropped his backpack and gave her a gentle hug. She returned his greeting and placed her hands on his head in blessing.

Dahlin saw that Marin had a meal prepared and ready on the table.

"I knew you would return today. Sit and enjoy this humble meal and tell me of your encounter with Rensin. I can see in your eyes that it went well," said Marin.

She gazed at him with a pure smile that shone in gentle beauty and cast an aura of peace within Dahlin's heart.

"Thank you for this wonderful meal. My stomach will enjoy its freshness after our long journey," laughed Dahlin.

After a few mouthfuls and a drink of water, Dahlin looked at Marin and told her of his battle with

Rensin. He described the light that flowed around him that prevented Rensin from harming him, and of Rensin's self-inflicted injury and healing, and his repentance. That they went back to Sunatin for Rensin desired to repair the damage he had caused his father, Johan, and to ask for his forgiveness. Upon reuniting them again, they secretly left Rensin and his father so that they did not interfere with their reunion. Perhaps later, he would return to visit them.

Dahlin paused in recollection, and Marin did not interrupt or break the silence.

"I wanted to ask you about the light that protected me from Rensin's sword. What was it? Where did it come from? I have never had that happen to me before," questioned Dahlin.

"You are a young Pentahaven, and you had just reached the age of awareness when you were kidnapped," replied Marin. "You missed the instructions on your awakening gifts. They came upon you, and you had to discover their meaning yourself. Even though you had lost your memory for a year, they were still developing inside of you. How did that make you feel?" asked Marin.

"It was very puzzling, but I felt I had to be cautious," replied Dahlin. "After your healing of my memories, I felt I knew more about what happened but still didn't know enough about the gifts," continued Dahlin.

"Learning about your gifts takes a lifetime," replied Marin. "Look at me. I am still learning even now, but I do know more as I am old," she said laughing.

"Old!" laughed Dahlin, "You are still so young to be old!" and they both laughed together.

"Your gifts and your intuitive abilities grow with you as you age. At first, they can be overwhelming once you realise the effect they have on others. You were wise to be cautious, which is a gift too. The light you experienced that protected you, is a visible sign of your gifts. You are one of only a few who have that ability. I have it but your parents don't. Your sister has it, but she hasn't become aware of it in her yet. She is younger than you, so hopefully you find her soon to guide her in their potential," Marin paused.

"I am so happy here and my family are suffering. I feel anxious for them," Dahlin felt a tear fall down his cheek.

"Do not be anxious, my dear Dahlin, but hopeful. I know you will find them and rescue everyone. But you can't go until you are ready. Do you feel that?" she asked.

"Yes, I sense that. Rushing in senselessly is surely the path of failure," replied Dahlin.

"Hmm you are getting very wise for someone so young!" laughed Marin with a gentle smile on her face.

This cheered Dahlin.

"I was wondering if this valley had a name. I can't recall it," he asked Marin.

"It will come to you. Just reflect for a moment and you will discover it and another name," she said in reply.

Dahlin smiled at her wisdom and closed his eyes for a couple of minutes.

"Of course! It is called Haven, that makes sense. And our town is called Havene, it is due west of here, only a day and a half walk," said Dahlin.

"Yes, that is correct. I suggest that when you start your quest, you visit Havene. You will find it deserted, as those who escaped capture are hiding in the surrounding area. They are too afraid to return to Havene. You will have to guide them back; it is in much need of repair," advised Marin.

"Yes, I will do that!" said Dahlin determinedly.

"I am pleased, but perhaps we need a little pause. Let's take a walk to see what your friends are doing," suggested Marin.

"Yes, a good idea. I was wondering about how they were fairing," agreed Dahlin.

As soon as they stepped outside, Animo, Intrepidus, Vigilans, Nobilis and Quaesitor raced over to Dahlin and Marin to greet them. Marin gave them all a cheery welcome.

Marin took Quaesitor and Nobilis around to the stable so that Dahlin could talk with the birds who had flown back to the orchard.

Animo, Intrepidus, and Vigilans flew over to Dahlin as he walked towards the orchard and landed on his outstretched arm.

"You seem a little downhearted my little friends," sensed Dahlin. "What is troubling you?"

The little birds flew over to a tree in the orchard and called their new friends to follow them back to Dahlin.

Dahlin sat down on a grassy hillock as the birds landed in front of him. He looked at his friends, then at their new friends. Animo, Intrepidus, and Vigilans hung their heads, not looking at Dahlin, and tweeted softly.

"Ah, I know what is in your hearts," interpreted Dahlin. "You want to follow me, but now you have found happiness in your new friends. You are torn between two choices. Well, I will make it easy for you. You have helped me in my journey, facing its dangers most remarkably. I am deeply grateful, and my heart loves you. But I will give you leave to stay here with your new friends in the safety of this valley. I expect more dangers on my next journey, and I wouldn't want you harmed."

The little birds flew to Dahlin's shoulders and stroked his face in thanks. They sang a joyful song, and their friends joined in, and it became a symphony.

"They sing so beautifully, Dahlin," said Marin as she returned from the stable.

"They have decided to stay here, and I am content for I know they will be safe," replied Dahlin.

"They are welcome, and I will take care of them when you are absent," reassured Marin. "Let's go back to the cottage for our supper. There are more things for you to know," continued Marin.

Marin prepared their meal as Dahlin stoked the fire. The warmth of the flames filled the room in unison with the warmth Dahlin felt in his heart.

After they had eaten, Dahlin sat on the rug near the fireplace and Marin sat on her rocking chair.

"Dahlin, have you thought about your gifts and how they have grown since your healing?" asked Marin gently.

"Yes, I was just pondering that," replied Dahlin. "When my little birds were troubled, I understood. When they tweeted to me, I knew what they were saying. I could talk to them, and they understood me. I sensed this a little before I came to the valley. But now it is stronger. I know what Quaesitor is saying when he neighs. When I fed him in the stable, he neighed, and I knew it meant, 'when are we going?' And when Nobilis came to say good night to me, he asked the same question. I said, 'soon'. And they both nodded."

"Your insights have developed abundantly and quickly. This, I believe, is due to their strength in you. I now know that you are one of the *intuitivus*, as am I. There are very few of us. Your parents are not strong in their gifts, neither are most of the Pentahavens. Their gifts lay dormant but will come to manifestation when needed or aided by an *intuitivus*. Your sister is like you but not aware of her gifts. You will have to awaken them in her," Marin paused to let this realisation enter Dahlin's heart.

Dahlin sighed.

"It feels like a great responsibility, but I sense no fear. I have assurance, hope and peace. A calmness," said Dahlin as he looked into Marin's beautiful blue eyes.

"That is how I feel," replied Marin. She smiled and laughed a little. "Did you know they can be diminished when necessary?"

"Diminished? What do you mean? I thought the gift would always be inside of me," questioned Dahlin.

"Yes, they are always inside of you. But sometimes you may need to minimise their affect or influence on others. You will know when you may need to do that. Here I will show you," replied Marin.

She closed her eyes and sighed and seemed to shrink, or at least Dahlin felt something like that. He looked at Marin and his feelings for her sank into an indifference.

"Stop that, it hurts," he whispered.

Marin opened her eyes and touched Dahlin on his cheek. Immediately he felt revived and held her hand tightly.

"That was desperate and lonely. My heart felt broken," he tried to explain.

"For you and me, the feeling is felt deeper," said

Marin. "Would you like to try?" suggested Marin.

"No, I do not want you to feel such sorrow. I know I can diminish them, if needed. Though it hurt, I thank you for showing me. The experience has taught me more about myself and the possibility of what I must do in the future," replied Dahlin.

"Thank you, my dear Dahlin. I knew you would say that," and she laughed. "I have felt much sorrow in my life, and in you, I only want to feel joy," responded Marin.

Dahlin thought for a moment.

"It explains now how, when I was hiding from Rensin in the dark outside his prison, he could not sense me. I must have brought it on myself," said Dahlin reflectively.

"Yes, that is probably true," agreed Marin.

They sat by the fire for another hour during which Marin sang Dahlin joyful songs. His heart felt enlivened. Marin went to her room to sleep and Dahlin fell asleep by the fire.

The next morning, Dahlin rose early and looked out of the window to see gentle rain falling. Over the Hermitage mountain a rainbow spread its beautiful seven colours – red, orange, yellow, green, blue, indigo, and violet. It was a sign of hope in the face of the danger he knew was before him.

He heard a noise and turned around to see Marin preparing breakfast. The gentleness of her movements amazed him. She did everything in perfect harmony. He could see her full of grace.

Marin had baked a loaf of bread, and when Dahlin ate some, he exclaimed, "This bread has a taste of sustenance more so than any bread I have eaten before. What has made it so special?"

"It has been made with my love. That is all I can say that has been added to its recipe," she laughed, and her eyes shone with light.

Dahlin spent another week with Marin. He rode Quaesitor and played with Nobilis. He trained them to bond as a team, work together, and sense each other's needs. He taught them to anticipate quickly and take swift action. These skills would be crucial for their future quest.

The following day, Dahlin kissed Marin farewell

and asked for her blessing. He knelt before her.

"There is no need to kneel before me. We are family, we are one," said Marin, unsurprised by Dahlin's humbleness.

"I choose to do so as an expression of my love and dedication to you," responded Dahlin.

"Then let it be so," replied Marin.

Before she could start her blessing, Quaesitor and Nobilis came forward and bowed before her too, seeking her blessing.

She lovingly looked at the three before her and raised her hands above them and chanted this blessing.

"I give you my blessing. I pray that the hardships that will come your way be met with courage and fortitude, but also with love. I pray that your quest to rescue our people will be successful but without the destruction of others, but instead, their reconciliation. Let light always be your guide," prayed Marin.

They remained still and silent. A light streamed down from the sky and embraced them, enveloping them in peace. They felt its presence, and it gave them resolve.

Time did not seem to pass.

The light lifted, and Dahlin, Quaesitor, and Nobilis rose to their feet. Marin kissed each of them.

"Go now, my rescuers. I will be watching from

afar," said Marin as a tear flowed down her cheek.

Dahlin wiped the tear away and hugged Marin one more time, then hopped onto Quaesitor's back, and they trotted away with Nobilis by their side.

☦ ☦ ☦

In the sky, a single black shape followed.

Milton Keynes UK
Ingram Content Group UK Ltd.
UKHW050218021124
450537UK00013B/73